"Do you know what you did wrong?"

Hannah stared up at Jake, sleepy-eyed with arousal from their kiss. "No."

"You don't just let a man do what he wants," Jake said. "You only let him deepen a kiss and get really intimate if that's what *you* want. If not, you have to stop him, shift your mouth or pull away, or he's going to think you want to get much more intimate, and he'll take it as permission to kiss you any way he wants."

"But what if he's one of the guys I want to kiss that way?"

"Then you kiss back." Jake stopped when he realized he was teaching her how to kiss. The thought sent a tingle of excitement through him until he reminded himself he was teaching her how to kiss so another man could enjoy her.

He was literally training her for his replacement.

Dear Reader,

We've been busy here at Silhouette Romance cooking up the next batch of tender, emotion-filled romances to add extra sizzle to your day.

First on the menu is Laurey Bright's modern-day Sleeping Beauty story, *With His Kiss* (#1660). Next, Melissa McClone whips up a sensuous, *Survivor*-like tale when total opposites must survive two weeks on an island, in *The Wedding Adventure* (#1661). Then bite into the next juicy SOULMATES series addition, *The Knight's Kiss* (#1663) by Nicole Burnham, about a cursed knight and the modern-day princess who has the power to unlock his hardened heart.

We hope you have room for more, because we have three other treats in store for you. First, popular Silhouette Romance author Susan Meier turns on the heat in *The Nanny Solution* (#1662), the third in her DAYCARE DADS miniseries about single fathers who learn the ABCs of love. Then, in Jill Limber's *Captivating a Cowboy* (#1664), are a city girl and a dyed-in-the-wool cowboy a recipe for disaster…or romance? Finally, Lissa Manley dishes out the laughs with *The Bachelor Chronicles* (#1665), in which a sassy journalist is assigned to get the city's most eligible—and stubborn—bachelor to go on a blind date!

I guarantee these heartwarming stories will keep you satisfied until next month when we serve up our list of great summer reads.

Happy reading!

Mary-Theresa Hussey
Senior Editor

Please address questions and book requests to:
Silhouette Reader Service
U.S.: 3010 Walden Ave., P.O. Box 1325, Buffalo, NY 14269
Canadian: P.O. Box 609, Fort Erie, Ont. L2A 5X3

The Nanny Solution

SUSAN MEIER

Daycare
DADS

SILHOUETTE *Romance*®

Published by Silhouette Books

America's Publisher of Contemporary Romance

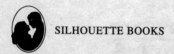

SILHOUETTE BOOKS

ISBN 0-373-19662-8

THE NANNY SOLUTION

This edition published by arrangement with Harlequin Books S.A.

® and TM are trademarks of Harlequin Books S.A., used under license. Trademarks indicated with ® are registered in the United States Patent and Trademark Office, the Canadian Trade Marks Office and in other countries.

Visit Silhouette at www.eHarlequin.com

Printed in U.S.A.

SUSAN MEIER

is one of eleven children, and though she has yet to write a book about a big family, many of her books explore the dynamics of "unusual" family situations such as large work "families," bosses who behave like overprotective fathers, or "sister" bonds created between friends. Because she has more than twenty nieces and nephews, children also are always popping up in her stories. Many of the funny scenes in her books are based on experiences raising her own children or interacting with her nieces and nephews.

She was born and raised in western Pennsylvania and continues to live in Pennsylvania.

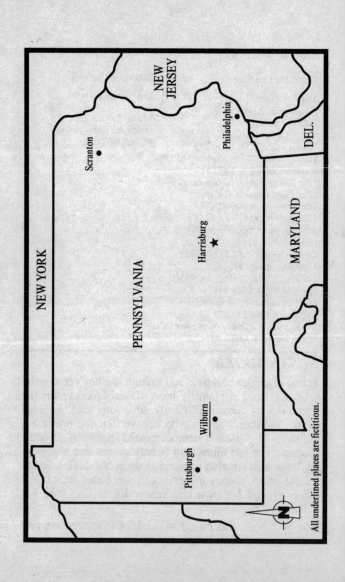

NEW YORK

NEW
JERSEY

Scranton
•

Philadelphia
•

DEL.

Harrisburg
★

PENNSYLVANIA

MARYLAND

Wilburn
•

Pittsburgh
•

All underlined places are fictitious.

Chapter One

"Can I have this dance?"

Hannah Evans faced Jake Malloy and his mouth fell open slightly. He had been expecting shyness and freckles from the baby sister of his best friend. Instead he found a woman's smile and skin as perfect as a sun-washed June morning. With her big green eyes, blond hair and shapely mouth, she was as classically beautiful as Lauren Bacall or Cybill Shepard.

His gaze involuntarily slid from her face, down the long column of her slender neck and to her breasts. The back of her black gown might have been the simple fare he expected from the former tomboy, but the front was not. Black lace cruised an enticing strip of white cleavage.

Something twisted in Jake's gut. When in the hell had Luke Evans's little sister grown up?

Jake's birthday guests mingled around them. The swish and rustle of satins and silks punctuated everyone's movements. Hannah smiled shakily. "I'm not much of a dancer…"

"Oh, that's all right." Jake took her hand, leading her onto the dance floor—which was really the living room of his huge home with all the furniture pushed back against the walls. The slide of her palm against his sent a frisson of awareness through him, and though this was his best friend's little sister, Jake didn't stop himself from enjoying it.

Besides, this was business. He hadn't asked Hannah to dance out of romantic interest, but because she was talking to Jake's former college roommate and current CIA contact, preventing him from leaving. While Jake and Hannah danced, Edgar Downing would slip out of the party unnoticed.

Just as they found a clear spot on the dance floor, the fast music stopped and the DJ shifted to a slow, romantic tune. Again, Jake ignored the twinge of conscience that this was Luke's baby sister. He wasn't interested in Hannah, only doing his job. He took her right hand in his and slid his left hand around her waist, pulling her close enough to make sure he kept her attention off Edgar and on him. The material of her silky slip dress felt soft and feminine against his fingers. He could smell her hair.

"So you're a teacher?"

She peeked up at him. Her long, straight locks shifted, slipped off her shoulder and cascaded down her back. They grazed the top of his hand. "I was."

He grimaced. "Sorry. I forgot Luke told me you got laid off. I didn't mean to bring up something unpleasant."

"Oh, that's all right."

Jake noticed that though she was talking and dancing, her eyes had begun to move again. He didn't think she was looking for Edgar. He believed it was a coincidence that she'd engaged his CIA boss in conversation the very minute Edgar needed to leave for another appointment. He suspected Hannah's lack of eye contact was the shyness he had been expecting to find when he'd first tapped her on the shoulder.

Not only had she always been a bit timid, but Jake was also nine years older than Hannah. Plus, he was quarterback of the football team that had won the state championship fifteen years ago. No team had ever come close to their record. Jake himself got a college scholarship out of it. When he graduated, he talked Troy Cramer, owner of one of the biggest software companies in the world, into forming an investment partnership. Troy put up the money and Jake investigated and chose the investments. Now Jake was also rich.

He was older, wiser, sophisticated, and in the small town of Wilburn, Pennsylvania, he was a legend. To a woman like Hannah, who hadn't even left home for college, dancing with him could be as intimidating as being asked to dance by Brad Pitt. Especially when her own life was in such a downturn.

"There's little point in trying to run from the truth," Hannah continued. "I got laid off thanks to some cutbacks. And I'm not the only one to get the ax, so everyone in town knows." She met his gaze. "Wilburn is too small of a place to run from things like that."

He wasn't prepared for the impact of staring directly into her pretty green eyes and didn't have time to brace for the bolt of lightning that sizzled through him.

He hid his reaction with a grimace. "I'm still sorry for bringing it up."

As if dismissing the topic, she returned her gaze to Jake's party guests. Her eyes once again surveyed the crowd. "I suppose I should tell you happy birthday."

"If you bought me a gift, that's happy birthday enough."

Just as Jake had hoped, his silly remark brought her attention back to him. "Very funny."

He smiled, continuing the teasing because he hated that she seemed so dejected. "It wasn't intended to be. I like presents."

"Right. I get it now. That's why you gave yourself a party."

"It didn't seem as if anyone else was going to give me one."

She laughed. "Then everything Luke told me about your vanity must be true."

"Absolutely," Jake agreed, tightening his hold on her waist, thrilled he had made her laugh. He knew he couldn't have her. He absolutely, definitely would not date the little sister of a man who knew the sordid details of Jake's love life. But that didn't mean they couldn't enjoy dancing.

Though the song was slow, he spun them around as if they were waltzing. He felt alive and wonderful and though he knew dancing with Hannah was part of the reason, the other part had more to do with Edgar recruiting him to work full-time for the CIA.

After eight years of being an Agency courier, someone who traveled so much that he could do pickups and deliveries for them, Edgar had approached him about becoming an agent. Not being able to shoot a gun and knowing absolutely nothing about covert operations, Jake had questioned Edgar's sanity in making the offer, but Edgar reminded him that he traveled so much that he knew certain cities like the back of his hand. He knew currency. He knew languages.

With that explanation, Jake had become unexpectedly interested. Not because he craved adventure—though he did—but because he was bored. So Edgar's offer appealed to him, and he told Edgar that if the CIA agent could show him he could handle this job, he would take it.

To prove to Jake that he could do this, Edgar had arranged for a more risky courier assignment. On Wednesday, Jake was to deliver a passport that had been sewn into the cover of the Day-Timer that Edgar had brought tonight as a birthday present. Jake would then "forget" the Day-Timer in a Paris café and it would be picked up by a waiter, who would drop it in the trash to be taken to a Dumpster behind the restaurant. An agent would pick it up and deliver it to the wife of an Iranian diplomat who had refused to defect until he had proof his wife was safe.

Though he hadn't yet fulfilled the assignment, Jake knew he could do it in his sleep and within a few weeks he would be on the CIA payroll. In spite of the fact that becoming an agent would probably mean he could have to quit working for Troy, Jake knew he had found the way to make his life interesting again. And that knowledge filled him with absolute joy.

"I don't mind being happy and confident. I'm lucky," he said, teasing Hannah again, making sure she enjoyed this dance as much as he did. "My life panned out beautifully. I have more money than I could ever spend. And I'm not too bad-looking if I do say so myself."

"You don't have to say so yourself," Hannah said, though her eyes were focused anywhere but on him. "Just hang around the bar. Most of the women there are talking about how attractive you are in that tux."

And she'd noticed. No wonder she wouldn't look at him. She didn't want him to see she found him attractive, too. "Well, I think that's only fair since I am the birthday boy. I should be the center of attention."

She snorted with disgust. "Right."

Jake laughed again, spun them around, but the song ended and Hannah quickly stepped away. Jake decided that was good. He liked her and they definitely had some kind of chemistry, but this was his best friend's little sister. If he as much as kissed her goodnight, Luke would probably punch him.

"Thank you for the dance."

"You're welcome," Hannah said, turning and scampering away from him.

Hannah Evans had no idea why Jake Malloy had asked her to dance, but she did know he wouldn't ask her again. Why? Because she was a dimwit.

Within two minutes of sliding into his arms, she'd had to admit that she had lost her job, which could only make her seem pathetic. Then to make matters worse, she couldn't keep eye contact because his eyes were so...well...powerful. Dark and focused, they glowed with the confidence of a man who had been around the world several times for business...and for pleasure. Even if she had dared to dream that he had asked her to dance because he was attracted to her looks—and from the once-over he had given her before he'd led her out to the dance floor, she had ac-

tually thought he was—she knew men like him pre-
ferred their women on the sophisticated side.

If there was one thing the regular citizens of Wilburn—including herself—were not, it was sophisticated. Wealthy residents like Jake and Troy Cramer,
who globe-trotted, had formal parties and mingled
with heads of state, were the exceptions, not the rule.
If Jake hadn't known that before, she had succeeded
in proving it when they'd danced. She had probably
also reminded him of why he didn't date women from
his hometown, even if he was attracted to them. Which
was why she had been pacing in the open area of the
powder room cursing her stupidity for the past few
minutes. She wasn't the kind of girl who had to be the
belle of the ball, but just once in her life she would
like to dance with the Prince without making a fool
of herself.

"Come on, Hannah. We're about to sit down for
dinner." Hannah's older sister, Sadie, had opened the
door and peeked inside. Dressed in a sleek pink gown
and dangling diamond earrings, Sadie not only
glowed, she also canceled Hannah's belief that all of
the residents of this town were unsophisticated. Sadie
had recently married Troy Cramer, the software billionaire, and from her chic outfit to her demeanor,
Hannah's sister was the picture of poise.

"Okay."

Hannah left the powder room and followed her sister down the hall. But the whole time she and Sadie
walked toward the party she stared at her sister wondering when this transition had occurred. Sure, Sadie
had gone away to college. She had attended the police
academy. She had also lived in an apartment in Pittsburgh and worked on the city of Pittsburgh police

force for five years. Hannah knew Sadie was a little more worldly than everybody else, but she hadn't noticed her turning into somebody who could fit in at a presidential reception. Yet, here she was.

"Let's go find Troy," Sadie said, gracefully maneuvering through the crowd and heading toward the French doors, directing Hannah to Jake's patio where a tent protected round tables that had been arranged for dinner. Covered in white linen cloths and decorated with fat bowls of fresh roses, the tables formed a large U around the pool. The June air smelled of blossoms.

The elegance of the house, the beauty of the grounds around it, and the casual romance of the night had Hannah almost sighing with longing, not so much out of desire for Jake's exquisite home as for the man who owned this wonderful place. Jake was handsome, masculine and vibrantly alive. He had as much charm and charisma as his wonderful estate. When she'd danced with him she would have happily cuddled closer—if only because he was irresistibly sexy. But, stunned by the impact of those dark eyes of his, she'd panicked, acted like a schoolgirl and blown any chance she might have had with him.

Sadie began guiding her to the table where Troy sat with Jake, and Hannah stopped abruptly. There was no way she was eating with him. None. She had already made herself look foolish enough. She wasn't adding to his already miserable impression by dropping a shrimp in her lap, which she would undoubtedly do if he gave her one of those looks again.

Before Sadie got too close to the table, Hannah indicated with a movement of her hand that she was about to go right. "I think I'll sit with Mom and Dad."

Pennsylvania's attorney general. In the not too distant future, Caro would be a political wife, dining in the governor's mansion.

How, in one short year, had all of her sisters changed so drastically?

Sadie's sandy-haired husband Troy restlessly rose from his seat. His black tux seemed to bring out the best of his blue eyes. To Hannah he looked the part of the successful, savvy businessman that he was.

"Are you guys going to stand there and whisper all night or are you going to sit down?"

"We're on our way to sit down," Hannah said to get everybody moving without informing Troy that she had no intention of sitting at his table. Especially now that she realized how far out of step she was with everybody else in her family. Sophisticated Sadie had billionaire Troy. Next month clever Caro would marry worldly Max. Even Maria, who had married young, had managed to become savvy and chic. They were perfect, beautiful, sophisticated women.

And somehow Hannah had missed the boat.

Jake began to chuckle over Troy's misery at being forced to endure two minutes away from his glowing bride until he noticed a whisper pass between Sadie and Maria. Suddenly he had the feeling Hannah's sisters didn't agree with his—and what he was sure would be vacationing Luke's—opinion of Jake steering clear of Hannah. From the continuing whispers, he was just about certain that Sadie and Maria were trying to match him off with their little sister!

"We're coming, darling," Sadie said to Troy with a sweet smile. Jake glanced at Hannah and their gazes met. Her big green eyes held his captive and he felt the same zap of electricity he had the first time she'd looked into his eyes tonight. All his man-attracted-to-a-woman instincts flared. He couldn't help it. There was something very sexy and very sensual about her tonight. Her eyes seemed to darken when she looked at him and he definitely knew she was attracted to him. Yet, she wasn't chasing him—*wouldn't* chase him. Actually, she kept running away from him.

Which was good because they were absolutely wrong for each other. Even if her sisters and his traitorous body would take issue with that right now.

"Is there room for Hannah to join us?" Sadie asked as she approached the table.

Troy pulled out the chair for his wife, and Jake rose, too. Just to keep things pleasant and to not arouse suspicion, he said, "Of course there is room for Hannah to join us."

"My parents are right over there," Hannah said. She met Jake's gaze again and enough sexual electricity to power New York City passed between them. "Thank you for the offer. But I would rather sit with them."

Jake almost breathed a sigh of relief because this situation was bad. Being attracted to somebody almost ten years younger was awkward enough, but knowing she was the baby sister of a guy who usually got details of his sexual…escapades…that was bad. Bad. Bad. Bad. She needed to sit at another table.

"Don't be silly," Sadie insisted, pulling out a chair for Hannah. Then she all but blocked her younger sister's path, preventing her from leaving.

"Just sit," Troy told Hannah, indicating the open seat with a nod of his head. "Sadie's not going to let you get away, anyway. No sense fighting about this."

"Right," Hannah said. Her gaze flitted to Jake's again and the electricity sizzled between them. He tried to blink away the connection, but it was useless. He was suffused with heat. He didn't have a clue why, but the way this woman looked at him seemed to turn him inside out.

"Excuse me, Mr. Malloy?"

Grateful for the interruption, Jake turned when the butler he had hired to supervise his party beckoned. From the corner of his eye, he watched Hannah succumb to the pressure of her sister and brother-in-law and take the seat across from his.

"Yes, Roger?"

"You have a guest."

Jake laughed. "It *is* a party."

Roger's eyebrows rose. "Well, that's true. But this one has a…package for you."

"Everybody here brought a package for me. We call them birthday gifts."

"Yes, sir. Very funny, sir. But if you would come out to the foyer, this could be explained much, much better."

Jake decided that was a great idea. He was sure that these few minutes away from Hannah would get rid of whatever kept causing him to feel all the wrong reactions to a woman he wasn't allowed to want. If that didn't work, he could simply stay away, pretend to be busy, until his head cleared and he could behave normally around her again.

"All right."

Jake turned to walk to the French doors but before he stepped away from the table, Felicity Lockhart, his red-haired, sex-goddess ex-girlfriend, flew onto the patio. Her eyes blazed and she carried a tightly wrapped bundle—his six-month-old son.

"Jake Malloy, we had a deal!"

Just like in the movies, the entire patio became quiet. Though Jake's first instinct was stunned surprise, he knew he could handle her. He always did.

"Felicity, it's very nice to see you."

She stomped her foot. "Don't you say it's nice to see me! You made a promise. Now you have to keep it."

"Okay," Jake said soothingly. "Honey," he added, slathering more balm on her bad mood. "Why don't you let poor Dixon out of the blanket so he can breathe? Better yet, give Dixon to me."

Felicity shoved Jake's son at him. Jake sighed with relief when he realized the baby was in a deep sleep. He cuddled Dixon against his chest before he faced his former girlfriend. "Where's Amanda?" he asked, referring to the nanny for which he paid through the nose.

"She's in L.A.," Felicity said quietly, as if she were calming down.

"And why would she be in L.A. when Dixon is in P.A.?"

"Because you promised me that if and when this day ever came we would not desert the baby to a nanny!"

Jake's eyes narrowed. "What day?"

She flailed her arms as if exasperated. "I am on my way to do the biggest movie of my life!"

"*You got a job?*" he asked incredulously, and realized too late that was the absolute wrong thing to do. Her blazing eyes heated two notches and her chin raised defiantly. It was the same expression she'd worn the whole time they'd argued about getting married. He didn't love her and she didn't love him, but he had been raised without his father and he wanted his son to know both parents.

"It isn't that I don't think you have talent," he quickly said. "Since Dixon was born, you just haven't really seemed all that focused on your career."

Luckily, his mother scampered over. Tall and regal in her gray-sequined gown, with dark hair and dark eyes, Georgiann Malloy reached for the baby. "Hi, Felicity!" she greeted in an overly cherry voice. Like Jake, his mother was a student of human nature and she knew how to handle people. "Why don't you give me the baby, and you two can go inside and talk about this privately."

"There is nothing to talk about!" Felicity shouted. "He promised and I am going." With that she turned and stomped her way off the patio and through the French doors into the house.

Jake's mother made a move to run after her, but Jake put his hand out to stop her. "Let her go."

"But…"

"Mom, I did tell her that I would take care of Dixon if she got a movie role and had to go on location."

"Yeah, but none of us ever thought she would actually get a movie."

"Well, she did and now I have a baby."

Hannah rocked back on her chair, her eyes wide with surprise, her brain shocked into numbness. *Jake Malloy was a daddy?*

"He's so cute," Sadie cooed, rising from her seat to rush over and fuss over the baby. "Jake, I'm so glad we finally get to see your son!"

"So am I!" Troy said. He also rose to look at the little boy Jake held.

Jake smiled sheepishly. "Yeah, well, even I hardly get to see him since he lives in L.A."

"Yeah," Hannah said, more to herself than to anyone else. Jake hadn't really kept his son a secret. Troy knew about him. Sadie obviously knew about him. Yet, Jake hadn't exactly made a public announcement, either. Could it be that perfect Jake Malloy wasn't so perfect, after all?

She smiled stupidly, feeling a relief of sorts that he was human. "This certainly puts Jake in a whole different light."

Hannah's sister Caro laughed. "Stop that," she said, patting Hannah's hand in reprimand. Not quite as tall as Hannah, but sharing her blond hair, Caro was the sibling Hannah most resembled.

"I didn't mean that to be rude," Hannah said. "It just came out wrong."

"I hope so," Max Riley, Caro's fiancé, agreed, catching Hannah's gaze with his striking blue eyes. "I would hate to have to break the news to people that you aren't the 'nice' Evans sister everyone believes you to be."

"The 'nice' Evans sister?" Caro and Hannah asked simultaneously.

"Yeah," Max said with a chuckle, as if it were common knowledge. "Maria is the mom. Sadie is the hottie. Caro's the smart…yet, gorgeous one," he said, sliding a meaningful glance in his fiancée's direction. "And Hannah's the nice one."

Hannah gaped at him. "Really?"

"Yeah," Max said.

Hannah had a little trouble digesting the fact that

she had been so neatly compartmentalized by her community, until she thought about her life. She was an elementary schoolteacher who had never left home. Not even for college. Her oldest brother, Dakota, had packed up for Massachusetts Institute of Technology and never returned, and she didn't want to risk hurting her parents like that. So even though her other brother, Luke, and her three sisters had at least left Wilburn to go to college, she had commuted so she could continue to help her aunt Sadie with her day care, so she could go to every family gathering, so she could attend Wilburn High football games.

Maybe she was "nice"? Maybe she was *too* nice? Maybe she was so stupidly nice and naive that she would trip over her tongue every time she danced with a handsome, sophisticated man like Jake Malloy!

"Maybe that's my problem. Maybe I've been nice too long."

Caro said only "Hmm" as she glanced over her shoulder.

Following the direction of Caro's gaze, Hannah saw that the baby had awakened and had nestled his face into Jake's neck.

Max said, "Looks like that little boy is very happy to be with his daddy."

"Yes, it does," Caro agreed. "And it looks like his daddy is also very happy to be with him."

Hannah frowned, wondering if the universe hadn't hiccuped or something. First, she realized the "niceness" she thought her best trait had probably been what was keeping her from becoming more sophisticated, then playboy Jake Malloy actually looked as though he loved being a father. From the way he walked around the patio showing off his baby to his guests, it was clear he loved the little boy and was proud of him.

Troy returned to the table and said, "That's one cute little boy."

"He is beautiful," Sadie said, joining her husband. "And he loves his daddy. The only problem is that Jake travels a lot for Troy."

Max shrugged. "So?"

"So, he's got a trip planned this week." Sadie leaned forward. "He's going to Paris, then Belgium."

"Oh!" Caro gasped. "He's so lucky."

"He won't be so lucky if he doesn't find a nanny," Jake's mother said as she and Jake's new stepfather, broad-shouldered investment counselor, Larry Simmons, walked to the table.

"Maybe we can help at the day care," Caro said at the same time that Jake, holding his adorable little boy, approached the gathering group.

Hannah had to admit the infant was sweet. Chubby-cheeked, with red hair, he didn't look a thing like his father, but apparently Jake didn't care. He held him as if he were his most prized possession.

"Jake," Caro continued, "I'm glad you're here. Your mother mentioned that you have to go out of town, and I suggested that maybe the day care could help out with Dixon. Aunt Sadie is back now. Her chemotherapy is over and she's nearly healthy as a horse. I'm working with her for backup."

"Thank you," Jake said, "but I think I need a nanny. My mother could easily watch the baby during the day like the day care, but won't be able to stay overnight," he added, casting a meaningful glance at his mother and her new husband. "So, it's overnight care I need. Somebody who can get up in the middle of the night with him, that kind of thing.''

Caro said, ''Why not hire Hannah?''

Hannah gaped at her older sister. ''What?''

Caro smiled. ''Well, the baby can't stay overnight at the day care and you're not working. It's not like you don't need the money. I seem to recall some school loans that aren't yet paid off.''

Ready to make an apology and an excuse for not being able to be his nanny, Hannah looked at Jake. But the oddest notion hit her. He needed a nanny, but she also needed something he had in abundance. Sophistication. If she were to live with him, even just to see *how* he lived, maybe she could change. She didn't exactly think sophistication would magically rub off on her, but she did have to start somewhere and seeing how the other half lived was definitely a good way.

''That might work,'' she said cautiously, and caught Jake's gaze. Again she felt the sizzle that always seemed to happen when their eyes locked. But, damn it, she didn't care. They might be attracted to each other, but he would never date her. One look at the woman he chose to be the mother of his son proved Hannah was not his type. And she would never date him. She knew when she was out of her league.

And she needed this. Tonight, she'd realized that her sisters had become a hundred times more sophisticated than she was. If she didn't catch up, she wouldn't fit into her own family.

Please, she tried to say with her eyes, since that seemed to be her best form of communication with Jake. *Please, hire me.*

Chapter Two

He should have told her no. Actually, he could have ignored her. She hadn't really asked the question with words, only with her eyes, so he could have easily pretended he hadn't seen. But something wouldn't let him. Caught in the gaze of those innocent green orbs, Jake found himself saying the word okay....

And then instantly decided he had to be absolutely insane. There was too much of a sexual attraction cracking between him and Hannah for them to be living under the same roof. As the person who cared for Dixon at night, Hannah wouldn't just be part of his household, she would be sleeping right down the hall from his own damned bedroom. It absolutely, positively, definitely would not work. Yet, once he said okay, his fate seemed sealed. Her sisters began to chatter. Troy started outlining details of her salary and benefits, and that was that.

Because of day-care commitments, Hannah couldn't start working for him until Monday morning, but Jake suddenly saw he could work that to his advantage. Instead of having his newly married mother help him and Dixon through the weekend, he decided he and his son would rough it and prove to everyone he could handle the baby himself.

Though he'd never had the baby at his house—only visited him at Felicity's, he and his mother had decorated a nursery and bought the appropriate baby furniture, so he had enough stuff and enough experience that he wasn't a complete idiot. Once he proved he could care for the baby alone, then even though Hannah would have to care for Dixon during the day when Jake was on trips, she wouldn't have to stay overnight when he was home. They wouldn't be sleeping a few doors down the hall from each other.

It seemed like an easy way to get himself out of his dilemma of living with a woman who held an unexpected sexual appeal for him. But when the baby threw up on Jake's clean shirt after his Saturday morning feeding, and cried nonstop for no apparent reason all Sunday night, Jake knew he couldn't handle Dixon alone. More than that, though, he suddenly found it easy to remember he was a grown man who had overcome sexual attractions before. This time he had the added incentive of knowing this particular woman was the baby sister—not just a sister but the *baby sister*—of his best friend. And if that wasn't enough, at a quarter to four Monday morning, he had to change one of ''those'' diapers.

When the doorbell rang at seven o'clock, Jake was done cursing his stupidity and was praising the heavens that his best friend had a sister who could help him.

''Hi! Good morning!'' he eagerly said as he opened

his front door to Hannah, who stood on his porch holding a suitcase and an overnight case. No woman ever
looked as good to him as she did at that moment. Not
because of her thick blond hair. Not because of the
dimple he saw when she smiled at him. Not even because her green eyes were sexy and alluring, but because he never again wanted to change another diaper.

"Hi," Hannah said, smiling at him as she entered
his foyer. She glanced around at the thick cherry-wood
trim, the crystal chandelier and the heavy desk that
decorated his foyer, looking naive and innocent and
so incredibly beautiful that Jake felt his breath catch.

With the memory of his weekend of baby trouble
ebbing away, and feeling like his normal self again,
Jake couldn't help but notice how naturally pretty she
was. Though the youngest Evans daughter had inherited the light hair, porcelain skin and full pink lips of
her mother's family, she had also inherited the long,
dark lashes from her father's side. She wouldn't need
make up. Her figure was so perfect, she could make a
sack look like Vera Wang.

Jake's breathing sharpened and pinpricks of awareness began to spike on his skin, but he stopped them
in their tracks with the reminder of the diaper.

"Where's the baby?"

"He's still upstairs. Not awake yet."

"Good. We can get me settled in my room. Then,
if you don't mind, I'll wake him, so we can begin to
get him on a schedule."

With the picture of the diaper still vibrating in his
memory, Jake smiled gratefully, the same way he
would with any assistant who was taking a messy job
off his hands. That was when he realized all he had
to do was treat Hannah like an assistant, a secretary,

or any other subordinate he was accustomed to dealing with and everything would be okay.

"That's fine," he said, taking the heavier suitcase from her and leading her up the stairs. "Do whatever you think we need to do to make our lives and Dixon's easier, because I have a feeling we're going to have him for a couple of months."

"Really? You heard from his mother?"

"I have a call in to his mother so we can get the details of the length of her shoot, but she hasn't called me back. If she doesn't phone by Wednesday, we'll know this commitment she forced on us is a lot longer than she wanted to admit."

Hannah laughed and Jake stiffened. He wasn't sure if it was a good idea to get too chummy with her. The goal here was to be polite and bosslike, not funny. Though, it was hard not to be at least a little silly about Felicity's antics. While dancing on Friday night it was clear he and Hannah shared the same sense of humor. Hannah would probably think it odd if they didn't laugh and tease and joke. Then she would figure out something was wrong, then she might go to her brother…

Yeah. Better let her laugh. No, actually, what he had to do was to continue to make her laugh as he had done on Friday night.

"Here's your room," he said as he opened the door. The floral bedspread and curtains seemed perfect for her, not just because the yellow and orange colors suited her but also because giving her this room put her an entire corridor away. He'd had to rearrange the nursery to do this but he knew moving Dixon was much better than sleeping two doors down from Hannah.

"You have your own bathroom." Which meant no awkward bathroom scene. No stockings over the shower rod. No running into each other naked beneath robes or bath towels.

"And here's the walk-in closet, with laundry chute and caddy." Which meant that as long as she put her clean and folded laundry on her shelf in the laundry room, she would only have to press a button to bring them to her room, not run around half naked looking for a blouse... Not that he thought she would. But he wasn't taking any chances.

"It's lovely."

"Thanks. My mother decorated it." He turned away from her and walked to the door, not about to stand and chat with her while she unpacked because that would definitely not be a bosslike thing. "I'll be in my office if you need me."

"Okay."

Jake closed the door behind him and sighed with relief. That had actually gone very, very well. He had to like her. He had to get along with her. She was his best friend's little sister, not to mention his boss Troy's sister-in-law. For the rest of his life, she would be popping up at parties, baptisms and weddings. He couldn't dislike her, avoid her, or ignore her. So all things considered, the first encounter had gone well. Plus, he was leaving for Paris this morning. She would have three full days to get herself adjusted to his house and he would have three full days to get himself adjusted to knowing she was in his house.

In his office, Jake typed in the short list of commands that activated his brand-new NannyCam and immediately the image of Dixon's nursery flashed onto his computer screen. He didn't feel guilty or feel as if he was spying on Hannah. To Jake this was simply a typical precaution any father who had to leave town the very first day of his nanny's employment would take.

Watching the scene of the white crib and changing table in the large airy room, made sunny and happy with the rainbow curtains that currently billowed in the morning breeze, Jake sat back in his tall-backed black leather office chair. He had only intended to turn on the system, but just then Hannah emerged from the adjoining bathroom, carrying the baby tub, which she set on a counter by the crib. She picked up squirming Dixon and set him in the water.

Jake leaned in to study the screen again. Clearly happy to be in his bath, Dixon gooed, bounced and splashed, but Hannah only laughed. Jake watched her, his head tilting to one side as he observed the way she handled Dixon.

''You better stop wiggling or you're going to slide right out of my hands.'' As she said that, she leaned down to Dixon and rubbed her nose against his. The baby giggled all the more. Enveloped in a warm, fatherly feeling, Jake smiled.

He couldn't picture Felicity doing this with his adorable little boy. Hell, he didn't think the L.A. nanny was this warm with Dixon. Yet, it didn't seem odd to see Hannah play so intimately with the baby she had gotten acquainted with at his party once they realized she would be his nanny. She and Dixon seemed at home with the playing, the tickling, the teasing.

He continued to silently watch Hannah, enjoying her interaction with Dixon, until he realized just how much he was enjoying it. He thought Hannah was pretty and sweet, and he adored his son. The sight of them together made him feel things that went beyond anything he had ever felt before and entered the soft, wonderful place he thought only existed in a man's imagination: the place where intimacy with a woman mingled with the joy of fatherhood.

He bounced away from the screen.

Whoa, he thought, then turned off his computer screen, though he left the computer itself on, to continue operating the camera and to record everything that took place in the nursery while he was gone.

That was a weird feeling.

A very weird feeling. Especially since he and Hannah had never been intimate.

It was the kind of feeling he had heard other men talk about with reference to their wives. The kind of feeling that scared him silly because listening to his friends talk about turning all mushy inside watching their wives with their babies made him think they were wimps. He could allow for a little wimpiness and sappiness about being a dad. He could let a guy get sloppy as all hell over a woman. But as soon as a man made that baby/mother connection, Jake knew it was all over for the poor sap. The guy was a goner.

And he did not intend for anything to be over for himself. He had a great life. He was rich. He was good-looking. He had any woman he wanted from the large, sophisticated circle of jet-setters in which he traveled. And, if everything went well with this week's delivery, he would have the kind of risky, adrenaline-producing career that most men only dreamed about.

He had no business thinking about mothers and babies. He loved Dixon. In fact, having Dixon was the blessing of his life because in spite of never marrying, he got to be a dad. He had an heir, money and, even if he only remained a CIA courier, a fabulous secret life of sorts. He didn't need to be thinking sappy thoughts about a pretty girl.

With that, he left his office and headed for the kitchen and a final cup of coffee before he departed for the airport. As he brought the cup to his lips, Hannah entered the kitchen, carrying a very clean, very nicely dressed Dixon. Wearing a pale blue T-shirt, shorts and little tennis shoes, Jake's six-month-old son already looked like the jock Jake was sure he would someday be.

"Here, give him to me," Jake said, reaching for his son.

"Be careful. He's particularly squirmy today."

"It surprises me that he took to you so well."

Hannah shrugged and gave him a beautiful smile that he felt the whole way to his toes. "It shouldn't. He's not old enough to make strange yet."

She issued the comment so casually that it struck Jake that part of the reason he was having more trouble controlling his feelings today was that Hannah was acting differently. He could have sworn she was afraid of him when he danced with her Friday night. Or, at the very least, that she was shy. But here she was behaving as if they were lifelong buddies.

He could easily believe she wanted to work for him because she had been laid off and needed the money. But that shouldn't make her eager to be around him. If anything, she should be shooing him out the door. Yet this morning he could swear she was happy to be with him.

As Hannah watched Jake cuddle Dixon affectionately against his chest, a quick round of realization buffeted her. First, he seemed suspicious of her and that could mean he sensed she was here under false pretenses. But that was only half true. Her main purpose might be to observe how he lived, but that didn't mean she couldn't take care of his son. Even analyzing Jake, she could effortlessly fulfill her duties as nanny.

Second, she really liked him. He was funny and, in spite of his wealth, he lived a relatively normal life. His house stood alone on the outskirts of town for privacy, but despite its size and beauty, it was a comfortable house. He was a comfortable guy.

Third, even though he was a jet-setting playboy, Jake made an adorable father. It was a role no one expected to see him play, but just as he did everything else in his life, he made fatherhood look easy.

But that was exactly why Hannah was here. She was sure it was sophistication that helped Jake make everything look simple and she wanted some of that sophistication. She didn't think just being around him would cause her to absorb the information and experience she needed, and she suspected that once they became better friends she would have to ask him questions. But that only reinforced that she had to be here. Seeing how the other half lived, making friends and asking questions to learn everything she could was Phase One of her new life plan. Phase Two was to get a job in Pittsburgh, once she had sophistication enough that she could ace an interview. And Phase Three was to actually move out of town.

She had to be here. If it killed her, she had to overcome his suspicions of her.

"Well, I'm off," Jake said. "There's a maid who

comes twice a week, by the way. Don't even rinse the dishes. Just take care of Dixon.''

"Okay," Hannah said, smiling at him as he kissed his little boy goodbye.

But when he stepped forward to hand the baby to Hannah, their eyes met and she didn't know how she knew, but she got the sudden impression he was thinking he should be kissing her goodbye too.

Heat suffused her. So did an awful need. He was absolutely everything any woman would want in a man, and he was within arm's distance. He also seemed to like her. Was it so hard to believe…

Damn it! She had to stop this wishful thinking! She could not be attracted to him. He was so far out of her league he would hurt her and there was no phase in her new life plan to accommodate getting over a broken heart.

She took Dixon from his hands and stepped back several paces. "Have fun in Paris."

Jake nodded once quickly, then bolted out the door.

Hannah breathed a sigh of relief. If she didn't behave herself, he was going to realize that she found him attractive and he would fire her and then she would be sunk.

"So, how did it go?"

Maria asked the question the very second Hannah stepped into the day care with Jake Malloy's little boy. But Maria wasn't the only Evans sister at their aunt's day care that morning, and Hannah knew the crowd hadn't gathered simply to help Aunt Sadie.

"How did what go?" she asked, being deliberately obtuse because she knew her sisters could be dangerous when they set their minds to something.

Sadie took Dixon, car seat and all, from Hannah's hands. "The thing with Jake, you idiot."

"There is no 'thing' with me and Jake except an opportunity for me to make money."

As Hannah said the last, her aunt Sadie came to the doorway where Hannah stood mobbed by her sisters. Tall and slender, dressed in blue jeans and a simple coral-colored blouse, she cut through the half moon made by the three women and effortlessly took Hannah's hand, turning her away from her sisters and toward herself.

"I'm so sorry that you lost your job."

Hannah smiled at her aunt. Her dark hair was growing back slowly in curly tufts, and her green eyes had a healthy sparkle that put everybody's mind at ease. Behind her, the play yards and toy boxes that symbolized Aunt Sadie's first love rimmed the open area used for games and naps.

"I'm going to be fine, Aunt Sadie. In fact, I have a plan."

"You do?" all three of her sisters said at once.

"Yes. I might be the baby of the family, but I'm twenty-four years old. An adult. Who can solve her own problems."

Hannah's sister Sadie set Dixon's travel seat on a changing table and began to unfasten the belts that held him secure. "So, what are you going to do?"

"Well, instead of using the money Jake pays me to make my student loan payments—" Hannah began, but Sadie interrupted her.

"Oh, Hannah, I forgot to tell you. On Friday night when Caro mentioned your student loans, Troy told me to tell you to round up your information and he'll pay them off for you."

"He doesn't have to..."

"He knows that. But he's got more money than he'll ever use and considers paying tuition and paying college loans as his part to help educate the country. He's happy to do it. Besides," Sadie said, laughing as she lifted Dixon out of the seat and gave him a smacking kiss. "If you don't give him the information, he has ways of getting it. He intends to pay off your college loans. You're not going to stop him."

"You know I'd rather try to pay them off myself, but I really appreciate his offer," Hannah said, realizing her sister was right. If Troy wanted to do this he would. Just as he had provided Aunt Sadie with financial security by giving her the day-care contract for the Sunbright Solutions employees he'd brought from California when he transferred his company to Wilburn, and just as he was currently building a new facility to accommodate them, Troy appeared to want to give her a start in life too.

"That actually speeds up my plans."

Caro took the baby from Sadie and nuzzled his neck. "What plans?"

"Jake's not going to have Dixon forever. So, being his nanny isn't a permanent job."

"You can work here," Aunt Sadie suggested.

Hannah smiled at her. "I know that, but I..."

"But you what?" Maria asked as she took Dixon from Caro.

"I want to leave town."

All three of her sisters gaped at her. "What?"

"I need to leave town. Look at you guys," she said, waving her hand in their direction. As comfortable in jeans and soft cotton blouses as they had been in evening gowns, her three sisters had shifted from being glamour girls to being mothers. Maria had her own children. Caro was helping Max raise his eighteen-month-old daughter Bethany. Sadie was mother to Troy's twins from his first marriage. Hannah could see Max's Bethany now, in the far corner of the playroom, being entertained by Troy's two eight-year-old daughters. "I'm not anywhere near like you."

Sadie gasped. "Of course, you are."

"No. I'm not. I've never been away from home. I want to be away from home."

Caro stared at her. "Really?"

"Yes."

"And I agree with her," Aunt Sadie said, taking Dixon from Maria who had just finished tickling his tummy. "I think if Hannah feels she needs to leave home, then now is the time."

"Well, now isn't exactly the time. I still need to get some money together. If Troy's going to pay off my loans, I'll save the money Jake pays me and in a few months I'll have enough to move to whatever town I can find a job in."

Aunt Sadie smiled. "I think that's a great idea."

Marie gave Hannah a concerned look.

Caro bestowed a confused expression.

Sadie Jr. crossed her arms on her chest and studied her.

"Forget about matchmaking me and Jake," Hannah said, putting an end to this once and for all. "I wasn't kidding when I said I thought he was too old for me." Hannah lied because she knew darned well he was perfect for her, she just wasn't perfect for him. If she admitted either of those things, her sisters wouldn't stop with their matchmaking efforts. "And I really feel strongly about leaving town so I can get some life experience."

Aunt Sadie said, "Good for you." Then, after nuzzling Dixon's cheek, she handed him to Caro again and left to check on the other children.

The second she was out of earshot, Maria grabbed Hannah's forearm to get her attention. "I don't mean to be the party pooper here, but I think your plan is all wrong."

"Why?"

"Hannah," Caro said, picking up where Maria left off. "You were the girl who didn't even leave town to go to college."

"That's my point…"

Sadie spun Hannah away from Caro. "But you love it here! And Jake is obviously attracted to you. You can't say you didn't notice the way he was looking at you at his birthday party."

"I didn't notice."

"Well, *I did!*" Maria said.

"So did I," Caro seconded.

"And I already said I saw it," Sadie said. "I think the guy is ready to settle down and I think that's why he kept looking at you Friday night. You're the kind of woman he could marry."

"You're thinking about leaving town because you want another teaching job," Maria said, taking Dixon from Caro. "But next year when the new budget is passed or when a few of the older teachers retire, you could get your job back. Until then," she said, placing a soft kiss on Dixon's cheek, "what if your job is here? What if Dixon is the reason Jake is ready to settle down? What if he's looking for someone to help him raise his son?"

Looking at adorable Dixon, something soft and warm floated through Hannah's heart. Just thinking about helping to raise the little boy gave her a fluttery feeling in the pit of her stomach.

"Yeah, and what if Jake's tired of slick women and is looking for a small-town girl?" Caro asked.

"I doubt that someone like Jake is interested in me…"

Caro chuckled. "I would have never dreamed I would end up marrying Max Riley… Yet here we are."

"Yeah, and me with Troy Cramer!" Sadie said then laughed. "The last I had heard he was a computer nerd. He surprised the hell out of me, and Jake might just surprise the hell out of you."

Hannah licked her suddenly dry lips.

Sadie caught her forearm and squeezed lightly. "Hannah, if you're attracted to him, you can't leave town without trying."

All right. So Hannah agreed with them. Sort of. Somewhat. It did seem possible that after fifteen years of running around, and also because he now had a baby, Jake might be ready to settle down. She could buy that.

Over the course of the three days Jake was away, Hannah also admitted to herself that she really didn't want to leave Wilburn. She never had. She liked it here. She liked the simple, quiet life. She liked kids. And, yes, damn it, she also liked Jake. If her sisters saw a spark of interest in his eyes then Hannah would be a fool to leave town without at least attempting a relationship with him.

After the cleaning lady had gone Thursday afternoon, Hannah popped a casserole into the oven, set Jake's dining room table with good china and waited for his return. The itinerary his secretary had given Hannah said that he would arrive in Pittsburgh at four and take Troy's private plane to the airstrip behind Troy's estate. Adding a twenty-minute drive from the airstrip, Jake would arrive a little before six.

But he wasn't home by a quarter to six as she believed. He didn't even make it home by six. Unfortunately, six turned into seven, which turned into eight, and Hannah had no choice but to put Dixon to bed. She lowered the temperature of the oven for her casserole and then began to pace the foyer. She considered calling the Sunbright offices to see if he had stopped there before coming home, but didn't feel right about that.

When another half hour ticked off the clock without Jake, Hannah began to worry in earnest. Troy had built the Sunbright Solutions complex in a wooded area. He'd wanted space to expand and plenty of land for employees to walk the grounds as they thought through complicated problems. But that also meant the road that led to the offices was twisty and windy. Jake could have been in an accident. He could have driven off the side of the road, rolled down a hill, landed in the thick forest and not be discovered for days!

She was just about to panic when the front door opened. Jake stepped inside as if nothing had happened and Hannah threw herself into his arms. "Oh, my gosh! I was so worried about you!"

For the briefest of seconds Hannah thought she felt his arms tighten around her, and she realized she was pressed against his chest. The stretch of her arms around his neck proved he was a good six inches taller than she was. She could smell the faint scent of the aftershave he had put on that morning.

Her breathing stopped. Every cell in her body sprang to life with awareness of him. And all she wanted at that moment was to snuggle against him and to bury her face in his neck.

But just as quickly as she had gotten the impression that his arms were around her, the feeling was gone. She realized that holding a briefcase and a suitcase made it impossible for him to hold her, yet she was clinging to his neck like an idiot.

She jumped away. Though her face flamed with embarrassment, she decided to use her brother's friendship with Jake to make hugging him seem reasonable. "Sorry. It's just that we never know about Luke. We're always pacing the floor, thinking the worst. I expected you at six and started to worry at eight. For the past half hour I've been pacing."

"I stopped at the office." Jake dropped his suitcase and pocketed his keys and, as if nothing had happened, turned toward the hallway that led to his office. "I work late a lot."

The completely neutral tone of his voice made Hannah swallow. Good Lord, she'd really made a fool of herself this time. She was such an idiot! Sadie would have never lost control and shown her emotions that way. Caro would have died first. Even Maria would have been cooler, calmer.

Hannah swallowed hard. "I made a casserole, if you're hungry."

He shrugged. "No. Not really." He began to walk down the corridor, paused, and faced her again. "You do know you're only here to care for the baby."

She swallowed, then nodded.

"You don't need to make me supper, wait for me, or anything like a regular housekeeper would do." He held her gaze. "You just take care of Dixon."

She nodded again. Jake smiled and resumed his trip to his office.

But tears stung Hannah's eyes. She was an idiot. A big, fat, stupid idiot! And if she didn't learn some sophistication soon and get the hell out of this town, she was going to die of embarrassment.

Chapter Three

Absolutely positive he was going to be punched out by his best friend in the very near future, Jake arrived at the Sunbright Solutions complex early the next morning. He had ducked out of his kitchen before Hannah had awakened and stopped at a convenience store for his morning coffee rather than drink it at home while he waited to say hello to Dixon. He was, admittedly, avoiding his new nanny until he figured out how to handle this mess.

He couldn't believe that Hannah had thrown herself into his arms the night before and all but wept with relief. Worse, he couldn't believe how elated he was to see her and how his arms had instinctively wrapped around her, even though he was holding a briefcase and a suitcase.... But she had leaped into his arms and he had wrapped his arms around her, and both had shocked him.

No. They had scared him. Sexually, he and Hannah were on the same page. He had many times seen the glint of attraction in her eyes that mirrored the intense gut-level reaction he kept having with her. That wasn't the problem.

The problem was that emotionally and experience-wise, he had her by almost ten years. There was no way in hell he could get involved with her. She was too young for him and, he reminded himself, she was the little sister of his best friend.

Unfortunately, neither of those points stopped the tingles, the urges, the unmitigated sexual response he had every time he got within ten feet of her.

Jake took the right, then the left that would get him in the corridor that led to the wing that housed the offices for his portion of the staff. Troy had been moving his company, Sunbright Solutions, from California to Wilburn for the past year. The first few months, employees who transferred worked in the office wing of Troy's mansion. Now that most of the Sunbright Solutions complex was complete, everyone had his or her own space. To Jake's great relief, there was little chance he would run into Sunbright's vice president of operations, Luke Evans, the big brother of the naive woman who seemed to have the hots for him.

Jake and Luke might have been on the same high school football team, but Jake was a quarterback and Luke was a fullback. At least fifty pounds—and the ability to bench-press large chunks of iron—separated them.

"Jake! Jake! Wait up!"

Jake squeezed his eyes shut as Luke's voice echoed through the sun-drenched glass corridor. So much for thinking twenty thousand square feet could save him.

He took a quick breath and turned to face Hannah's big brother. He didn't like the urgency of his best

friend's tone. Jake liked even less that while he had
been globe-trotting, still had jet lag and had spent his
first night home worrying about his attraction to this
man's sister, Luke had been sleeping in his own bed,
and visiting his gym. His green eyes were clear and
rested. His broad shoulders filled out his navy-blue suit
coat in the way that spoke of commitment to regular
strength training. If Luke asked about Hannah and
Jake said the wrong thing, one jab would send Jake
sprawling.

"I have a few questions to ask you about the California complex."

Jake almost choked on a sigh of relief. "Okay,
shoot. Talk to me while we walk."

"I'd rather we kept this just between us. Let's make
small talk until we get behind a closed door."

"Problem?"

"Let's wait for the door."

"Okay," Jake said, getting the message. "So got
any plans for the weekend?" Though the question was
trite and even somewhat stupid, he tossed it out
quickly to prevent Luke from asking about Hannah.

"Nothing special. The usual stuff," Luke said with
a laugh, undoubtedly at the stupidity of the question.
Then just as Jake expected, he asked, "How is Hannah
working out?"

"Oh, fine. Great." Pretending to be juggling his
takeout cup of coffee, Jake averted Luke's gaze. He
couldn't risk that Luke would see something—anything—in his eyes. Men usually weren't known for
being observant, but Jake had never dealt with an older
brother before. God knew what a man could see in
another man's eyes when it came to his sister—his
baby sister.

"I'm not talking about her work as your nanny, I was actually wondering if you noticed anything odd about her."

"I didn't notice anything odd," Jake said as he deliberately juggled his coffee again so it would spill out of the crack in the plastic lid, and he could continue to pretend to be more interested in his coffee than the conversation.

"She isn't talking about stupid things?"

"Women always talk about stupid things," Jake said. He knew Luke would expect that kind of comeback and now was not the time to act out of character.

Luke laughed. "Right. You should hear my sisters lately," he said, then shook his head. "That's actually why I'm asking. Ever since Aunt Sadie's home and fully recovered, my sisters have been looking for a new mission, and I think Hannah is it."

Jake paused, his heart nearly stopping. At his birthday party he had sensed the same thing. He believed they were matchmaking him and Hannah. For all he knew they could still be.

Dear God, this just kept getting worse.

Not wanting Luke to get suspicious, Jake began to walk again. "Well, for what it's worth, Hannah is a fabulous nanny. She doesn't look to have any problem to me..." *Except that she's infatuated with me and I'm not sleeping because I want to make love to her...* "And I will keep an eye out for her while she's at my house."

Because he would. He wouldn't tell Luke that the person Jake should be protecting Hannah from was himself. That would certainly earn him a punch in the face. But Jake would protect her from himself. That was the right thing to do.

"To tell you the truth, I'm sort of glad she's at your house and away from my other sisters. Their hearts are in the right place, but I think they just don't get it with Hannah. She's been sheltered, protected, by all of us too long. Getting laid off from her teaching job might be the best thing that ever happened to her, because it might just force her to take a big step. Instead of any one of us nudging her down any road, what she really needs is to be out on her own. To experiment. To cut loose and do something spirited. Something wild."

"Right," Jake croaked.

"Anyway, I'm glad you're looking out for her."

"Oh, yeah. Of course I'm looking out for her."

They stepped into Jake's office. Luke closed the door and the discussion shifted to Luke's questions about the sale of the California complex for Sunbright. But that didn't stop Jake from sweating.

Jake managed to find projects to keep him busy enough that he didn't get home until after seven that night. Because Hannah wasn't anywhere around, he sneaked back to his office and immediately flipped on the NannyCam. Just as he expected, she was in the nursery. She had Dixon on the changing table and was preparing him for his bath before bedtime.

"You are such a cute little boy," she crooned, and Jake relaxed in his chair. *This* was what he wanted from her.

"When you grow up, you're going to be every bit as handsome as your daddy."

That was not!

"But he's such a stick in the mud, pain in the butt," she said, lifting Dixon and set him in the baby bathtub, which was setting on the counter by the changing table.

The camera was so good Jake could see the shift and movement of her breasts beneath her lightweight cotton shirt. He cursed himself for looking and forced himself to watch the bounce of her long yellow ponytail as she lifted and settled Dixon.

"He doesn't want to do anything I want and if he doesn't soon fall in line, my whole purpose for being here is going to be moot!"

Jake loosened his collar. He didn't need to think about what she meant. She was probably talking about that cutting-loose-doing-something-wild thing Luke had referred to earlier. And she wanted to do it with him. His breathing got shallow. His blood raced through his veins.

"All I need is for him to talk to me a bit more. To explain some things to me."

Huh?

"It's like this, Dixon. Wilburn is a great place. Truthfully, I would live here forever if I could. But I can't. I lost my job."

The baby giggled and splashed his hand in the water. Jake leaned closer.

"I need to go to Pittsburgh to work. But I can't go to Pittsburgh as a bumbling idiot…"

She wasn't a bumbling idiot!

"Unless I learn how to talk to people, I won't even get a job because I won't pass an interview." She ran a cloth along Dixon's tummy, then over his shoulders and down his back.

Jake frowned. What made her think she wouldn't pass an interview?

"How do I know I won't pass an interview?" she

asked the baby, who only giggled. "Because people misinterpret me. I can tell by the way your dad looks at me that he gets the wrong impression from everything I say and do."

Jake leaned back in his chair. *Ouch.*

"It's not like I need lessons or anything. I honest to God think I could get a lot smarter and or maybe behave a lot less like a country bumpkin, if I just could sit and talk with him every night until your mom gets back. I could lose my nervousness around sophisticated people and maybe learn a thing or two if he would tell me about the places he's traveled. That's all I want. Just to talk to him."

Jake leaned back in his chair again. Well, all righty, then. She didn't like him. Well, she did "like" him. She simply wasn't attracted to him. Not the way he was to her. It was a punch to the solar plexus, but he could handle that. Particularly since it would keep him from getting a punch in the nose from his best friend.

He thought about the conversation he had had with Luke that morning and realized that what Luke was sensing in his little sister wasn't a need to do something wild or to cut loose. It was a desire to grow and mature, and it was compounded by the fact that she felt she needed help. She wanted to get away, and was even planning to go away, but she knew she wouldn't make it away from home unless she became more worldly, so she was looking for someone to help her. That was what Luke was seeing, and that's why all his brotherly instincts had sprung to life. Her quest for someone to teach her things made her vulnerable.

Luke might not even realize it himself, but Jake suspected he was worried about Hannah because if the wrong guy found her when she was in this confused mood, Luke understood exactly what could happen. Hell, *Jake* understood exactly what could happen. An unscrupulous man could take advantage of her.

Jake knew he had to do something. He couldn't sit by and let the situation unfold naturally. If he did, things could get ugly.

He decided he had to be the one to give her lessons. And he did mean *lessons*. He understood that she felt just talking to him might help her, but the truth was he wanted the forum to warn her about guys like… Well, guys like him. She was too pretty and had a natural sensuality that would attract all the wrong men. Like a karate instructor, he wanted to be able to talk about the possible attacks and to show her the countermoves.

The only question was, how? How could he bring it up without letting her know he had seen her on camera?

He watched her finish Dixon's bath, then turned off the monitor and met her in the kitchen. She had the little boy in a traveling seat that could be set on the table. She reached into the cupboard for a jar of baby food and inspiration struck.

"You know, Hannah," he said, and waited for those innocent green eyes to raise until they met his gaze. "I really love Dixon, and I do the absolute best I can with him. But I'm not quite as good of a dad as I need to be."

"Oh, you're fine," she said, dismissing him, and Jake wondered how in the world he could have ever thought she was attracted to him.

"No. Actually, I'm not fine. Well, maybe I am *fine*. But I'm not exceptional. I want to be exceptional. I was thinking that you could teach me."

She caught his gaze again. In spite of the fact that he now knew she wasn't attracted to him, Jake felt his blood heat. She was just too darned pretty for her own good.

"Teach you?"

"Yeah, I don't have time to go to the single dad classes your aunt Sadie has, but they are a really good idea."

"Yes, they are."

"But I don't have time."

"So you said."

"So I was thinking that maybe there was something you and I could barter for lessons. If you would be willing to teach me, I would be willing to do something for you in return. Like teach you something. I want this to be a payment other than money since I'm already giving you money to care for Dixon." He held her gaze. "Is there something I could help you with? Something I could teach you?"

He watched the light of hope come to Hannah's eyes. He watched her think it through. The whole time he internally crossed his fingers, held his breath and tried telepathically to get her to say yes.

Finally she said, "Well, truthfully, there is something I need to learn."

"I would be happy to do whatever I could," he said in a rush, hoping she wouldn't change her mind. His own reactions to her—even knowing she didn't like him, even knowing her brother would sock him if he touched her—were evidence to him that every man in the world would be after her once she left her little hometown. And the guys who would get into the door of her apartment, get her into the back seat of a car or get her into their apartments were the ones with all *his* lines. He had to protect her.

She took a long breath. Jake held his. *Please.* This time he begged the message with his eyes. *Please let me teach you this.*

She sighed. "Okay, here goes. I want to move away. But I can't go until I get a little smarter about things."

"A little smarter about things?"

She nodded. "Yes. I want lessons in how to be cooler, more…you know…with it."

"You mean, sophisticated?"

She grimaced. "Yeah. I'm not quick on my feet, and I'm afraid I'm going to make huge mistakes when I go to Pittsburgh and interview for teaching jobs there."

"I can help you with that," Jake said, but inside he was getting nervous again because she wasn't giving him enough leeway to teach her what she really needed to learn. He wanted to help her with the important stuff. The stuff that would cause her brother Luke to walk to Pittsburgh and beat the snot out of any man who took advantage of her. He wanted to prevent any man from taking advantage of her.

She took another long breath. "I also realize I'm very naive about men. I don't want to get into any bad situations in that way, either. I would really like some…not really dating lessons…but maybe some pointers about city guys. You know, guys that are going to say and do different things than the guys I went to school with."

And the guys who knew your big brother would kill them if they touched you, Jake said in his head as he silently breathed his sigh of relief.

"Okay. I'm your man," he said so gratefully that he nearly forgot this was supposed to be a fair exchange. "That is if you're willing to teach me how to take better care of Dixon."

"If you want to learn how to care for Dixon, you have to start coming home earlier. You leave right after he gets up, and half the time he's in bed when you get home."

"Fair enough, but that means we'll have to add making dinner to your job description, and we'll have to eat together every night," Jake said, nearly smirking at the clever way he slid in the one real request she had mentioned to Dixon. "Not only will I miss the dinner meetings Troy sometimes holds in our cafeteria, but I could teach you a lot over a meal."

"I can do that," Hannah said happily, but something didn't feel right to her. She didn't exactly feel conned, but she didn't exactly feel that everything was normal, either.

Jake stuck out his hand to shake hers and Hannah took it. The second their palms touched she felt the zing of electricity and she knew why this bothered her. She liked him and was attracted to him. She would always like him and always be attracted to him and she had just asked him to help her get ready to find another man.

If anybody was conning anybody here, she was conning him, and that's why she felt so funny about it. Still, given that he didn't like her, it wasn't as if she was cheating him. Plus, she planned to give him such good lessons that their trade would be even. And she was making dinner for him. Not something in her job description.

She spent the next day convincing herself that this

was a fair exchange and did such a good job of it that when he arrived home that night she was ready. Even before they ate her pot roast, which turned out to be ungodly dry, she edged him upstairs to do his daddy duties.

"Okay, here's the deal," she said as they climbed the steps. "You were late, which means that Dixon is already bathed and ready for bed."

"Sorry. I have to admit that before we agreed to all of this, I sort of hung around and attended meetings that I really didn't need to attend, but today's holdups were legitimate."

"That's okay. It shows you're learning. You could have come home early yesterday and didn't, but tonight taught you that you have to take advantage of the times when you can come home."

"Yeah," he said, agreeing that he had learned his lesson.

"Let me tell you something, Jake. From my dealings with fathers of the children I taught at Wilburn Elementary, and fathers I saw at the day care, I know that men don't have a lot of natural instincts when it comes to planning ahead with kids. This is one of those things you're going to have to learn."

"What you're really saying is that I'm not a louse."

Hannah laughed at his self-depreciating tone. "Absolutely. You're just a victim of nature. But we can fix that. We can overcome nature with common sense and a good plan."

They stepped into the nursery where Dixon lay in his crib, playing with a mobile.

"So what's the good plan?"

"You have to learn that your first stop when you come home should be here."

She pointed to the singing baby lying in the crib, kicking to get his dad's attention. "All day long he's missed you."

Jake gave her a skeptical look. "Really?"

"Yes!" She nudged his back to get him to go to the crib. "He might be a baby but he knows you. He knows you are the special person in his life. That's *his* instinct."

"So he's been waiting for me all day," Jake said as he leaned in and took Dixon from the crib. The baby immediately slapped his face.

Hannah laughed. "Yes. That slap is actually his way of showing you love."

"Right."

Jake hugged Dixon and the baby responded by wrapping his arms around his dad's neck. Jake seemed to do very well with the baby once he remembered to spend time with him, and Hannah decided the real thing Jake had to learn was that he was Dixon's primary caregiver. She didn't need to interfere with any other part of his routine. So she let him and his son have a minute to say hello. As she watched them cuddle while Jake said stupid, inconsequential baby things, her chest tightened.

If nothing else, Jake's intention to learn how to care for his son was sincere. Clearly he loved this little boy. Clearly he wanted to be a good dad.

But she still felt odd. As if something wasn't quite right.

"Okay, now, before we put him to bed, we need to check his diaper one final time."

Jake peeked at her. "*I* should do that?"

"Yes."

"Really, that's the big reason I hired you."

Hannah laughed. "No, you hired me to care for him overnight and while you're gone."

He grimaced. "Right."

He obviously didn't want to change the diaper but, like a trooper, laid the baby on the changing table and did his duty. When he discovered only wetness, not messiness, his relief was audible.

"It must be my lucky day."

"It must be," Hannah said, leaning forward to watch him. He met her gaze and smiled at her, and Hannah's heart knocked against her ribs. It wasn't a sexual smile. It wasn't a come-on smile. It was a smile between friends and in some ways that was all the more dangerous. Because she liked him she could easily misconstrue that smile…

But really, Hannah thought, could you "misconstrue" a smile between friends? A smile between friends wasn't an acknowledgment of affection. It was an acknowledgment of friendship, companionship, a meeting of the minds. And, technically, there was nothing wrong with being friends, nothing wrong with him liking her.

He finished the diaper and breathed a sigh of relief. "Okay, I'm feeling like a daddy now."

"I think you're a really good dad."

He smiled and looked at her again, but when their gazes caught he seemed to freeze in place. The expression in his eyes changed from that friendly acknowledgment of a few minutes ago to male/female awareness. Just like at his birthday party, sexual electricity raced between them. Except this time they were friends. This time it wasn't just chemistry. This time what they felt for each other had some substance.

Obviously wanting to break the spell, he turned to

put Dixon in his crib. But he had stared at her long enough that she knew the truth. In spite of all the signals he had been giving her to the contrary, he was attracted to her. Unfortunately, the way he turned away also reminded her that he didn't want to be.

"Ready for bed?"

The little boy giggled.

Jake laid him in his crib. And Hannah watched it all. Though she tried to control it, a feeling of love overwhelmed her because not only did she care about both Dixon and Jake, she also wanted Jake to be the best dad he could be. Not just for Dixon's sake, but for Jake's, too. She didn't want him to have any regrets over missed memories.

She was so lost in thought that she didn't notice when Jake turned away from the crib, and he bumped into her. She paced back instinctively as Jake caught her upper arms. She halted her backward progress, waiting for him to release her, but he never did.

Her eyes rose until they caught his gaze. The way he was looking at her made her mouth go dry. He had wonderful eyes. Dark. Piercing. And the message he was sending her was the message her sisters told her they had seen all along. He liked her. He liked her as more than a nanny. More than a friend. He might not want to, but he did.

Desire kindled in her middle and began to seep through her along with a giddy kind of joy. He *wanted* her. He couldn't stop himself from wanting her.

They stood staring at each other for several seconds, until, as if mesmerized or hypnotized, he bent and touched his lips to hers.

A lightening bolt of sensation thundered through Hannah. Sweet, syrupy heaviness weighed down her limbs. The words of her sisters echoed in her head. What if he was ready to settle down? What if that was why he kept looking at her oddly? What if he was seeking someone to help him raise his son? What if he really was done with slick city women and was looking for a small-town girl? What if he just didn't know how to go about setting things in motion between them? Or, worse, what if, in her inexperience, she kept misinterpreting him?

Then she would be a fool to let this opportunity slip away.

She opened her mouth and kissed him back, tentatively at first, expecting, still, that he would change his mind at any second, or tell her she had somehow misinterpreted him. Instead he deepened the kiss, letting his tongue tumble into her mouth, and pulling her closer with his strong arms. Hannah's breath shuddered out on a sigh that echoed from her to him and the kiss deepened, lasting for dark, delicious moments. Want and need became the same thing. The desire in her middle became a full-fledged fire. A fierce explosion of shivers overtook her. And she realized *this* experience was why her sisters were different and *this* experience was what she needed to learn about to take the next step in her life. But as quickly as she made that conclusion, Jake jumped away from her.

"Finish with Dixon," he croaked, then bolted out of the room.

Chapter Four

Jake waited nervously for Hannah to return downstairs. With his lips still tingling from her kiss and wanting more, he knew he had made a big mistake. Being in such close quarters was killing him and confusing him, but when he sifted away all the physical longings and emotions that made no sense, he did know the bottom-line right thing to do and he was about to do it.

"I can't like you," he said without preamble as she walked down the steps.

Light from the crystal chandelier danced off her golden hair. Her modest shorts and T-shirt were somehow sexier than a nightie. Just looking at her, all Jake's reasons for wanting her came flooding back. Luckily, all his reasons for not being able to have her chased them away.

"First of all, you're ten years younger than I am."

"Nine, Moses." She finished her descent and led

him into his living room. "I'm only nine years younger than you are."

"All right, nine." Her sense of humor about the situation almost did him in. But he wouldn't let himself laugh. He certainly wouldn't let himself enjoy her. *That,* he now realized, was mistake number one. She was so sweet and so much fun he kept letting his guard down. Then her goodness would sneak up on him, and his unexpected enjoyment of that innocence would confuse him. And then—whoosh!—in washed attraction and he was feeling things he had no right to feel.

He cleared his throat. "Even if you don't agree that the age difference makes us incompatible, you can't forget that I'm your brother's best friend."

Her face scrunched in confusion. "You would let my brother keep you from liking me?"

"Let me put it this way. *I* wouldn't do anything. It's what you brother would do to me. Luke knows details about my—" unsure of a euphemism for the escapades he had had with women he finally settled on "—*dating life* that he might consider make me an inappropriate companion for you. And if I were to pursue you—hell, if Luke were even to find out that I kissed you—he would probably kill me."

"Oh."

"Yeah, oh."

Jake saw from the expression in her pretty green eyes that that explanation was sinking in and he thanked his lucky stars. Not just because he wanted to keep his sanity and his best friend, but also because he couldn't tell her the biggest reason that they couldn't be together. His last delivery for the CIA had gone so well that he had been cleared for undercover assignments, which could be dangerous, and that precluded him from becoming permanently involved with anyone. But more than that, he couldn't tell her about his association with the CIA, and that wasn't the way a man forged an honest relationship with a woman.

Felicity had already told Jake his globe-trotting for Troy made him a horrible candidate for a husband, but his new job, which required him to travel even more, sealed the deal. He didn't want to be like his dad and marry a woman then desert his family to his career. He knew firsthand that wasn't fair and what kind of damage that could cause.

More than that, though, working for the CIA, Jake finally felt as though he had found his calling, his purpose, his reason for being on this planet at this particular point in history. With a workaholic dad he never saw and then eventually lost to death, and a mother who seemed to have to work herself silly just to put food on the table, Jake had always wondered why the heck he was here. He could play football. He could spot a good investment. And he could certainly make money. But he didn't have any sense of purpose until Edgar recruited him only a few weeks before.

He unexpectedly wished he could tell Hannah that. Not just because it would make more sense as the explanation for why they shouldn't even dabble in kisses, but because of all the people he knew, she was the one who would get excited about his new job. She wanted more out of her own life than what she had and she was willing to go to unusual methods to get it.

Yeah, she would understand.

When he drew the parallel between her life and his, Jake recognized he was in bigger trouble than he thought. He had begun thinking of her in the way he thought of people like Troy and Edgar, trusted confidants. And that was wrong. Wrong. Wrong. Wrong. She was not a trusted confidante. She was his nanny. His best friend's little sister. An innocent elementary schoolteacher who needed his help. He had to remember that.

"When it comes to romance, I'm an idiot," he said finally, hammering the last nail in the coffin for their potential relationship, because if he gave her one iota of hope, she would end up getting hurt and he didn't want to hurt her. "I'm not the kind of guy who will settle down. Ask your brother about some of the things I've done, and this time tomorrow you'll wonder if it's even wise to work for me."

With that he left the room and headed upstairs, feeling like hell because he had to leave with her believing the worst of him. But, he supposed, that was poetic justice since he deserved to feel pretty crappy for kissing her when he knew he had no right to.

The next morning, as Hannah prepared Dixon for his bath, she went over everything Jake had said the night before, and every time she felt even dumber. As if it wasn't embarrassing enough to be falling for a man who was all wrong for her, said man had felt the need to spell out the reasons why they shouldn't have a relationship. Obviously the thing she said or did that made him bolt from the room also made him believe she wasn't capable of figuring it out for herself.

Proof again that she needed to smarten up—and quickly—or she wouldn't survive life in the city. The only good thing about this situation was that she had already embarrassed herself completely in front of

Jake. Nothing she did after this could make her look any worse.

She hoped.

As was their typical morning routine, after dressing Dixon she took him to the kitchen for his breakfast. She slid him into his high chair, and Jake arrived. He mumbled a hello to her, gave Dixon a smacking kiss on the cheek, then turned away and reached for a coffee mug. His white shirt highlighted the tan skin of his neck and hands, reminding her that this was a guy with a year-round tan, not because he visited tanning beds, but because he spent a lot of his winter in the Mediterranean. His life was so different from hers that it was astounding they even had anything to talk about. And her brother was his best friend. And getting involved with her would get him into trouble.

It was no wonder he was annoyed with her for being attracted to him.

She cleared her throat.

He peered over at her.

"I know you're mad at me," she said.

"I'm not mad. I'm…"

She stopped him with a wave of her hand. "All right, you're not mad. You simply don't want to have anything to do with me so you made sure last night that I wouldn't want to have anything to do with you."

From the expression on his face, it gave him a great deal of relief that she understood that. "Right."

"Okay, so now we're on the same page. You're not interested in me and I would be an absolute idiot to be interested in you…"

"Hannah, I…"

She stopped him again. "Let me finish. I can't be

interested in you. I can't risk alienating you because I need you.''

His eyes narrowed.

"Jake, you see how naive I am! If you don't help me, I'm not even going to get a job. I won't make it through an interview at a big-city school.''

"Hannah, I don't think you're that bad.''

"I don't want to be even a little bit bad. I want to go to the city and have a nice life. A fun life. Come on, Jake! You didn't settle! You're doing everything you want. I want to have a fun life like yours.''

His eyebrows rose. "No way am I showing you how to have a life like mine!''

"All right. Maybe that's a little extreme, but I at least need to get a job, and I don't think I'm going to if the discussion we had last night means we're breaking our deal and we're not going to help each other.''

He sighed.

"*Please* say we're not breaking our deal and that you're still going to help me.''

He pointed his index finger at her. "You know, we've got to stop doing this to each other.''

"What?''

"Begging each other. We use the word please like a weapon.''

"Okay, I agree I won't say please anymore, if you agree to help me.''

"I can't help you.''

"You have to! I'm so naive about men that if you don't help me, I'm going to make a fool of myself.''

"Everybody makes a fool of themselves once in a while…''

She shook her head. "Not the way I will. I don't want to go to Pittsburgh looking like and acting like everybody's kid sister and getting myself into situations where men get the wrong idea because I'm too dumb to know I'm giving them the wrong idea. Do you see what I'm saying?''

Yeah, he saw exactly what she was saying. She wanted him to teach her things to protect herself from men like him. Peachy. That made him feel swell.

''I have to learn how to flirt the right way, say the right things, *do* the right things to get the *right* men to like me.''

He sighed.

''And you're back to falling short with Dixon. I noticed you weren't in the nursery with us this morning.'' She paused and inhaled a long breath. ''So I will be very happy to continue to teach you how to be a good dad, if you will teach me some stuff to protect me from the wrong men and help me entice the right ones.''

He squeezed his eyes shut. ''Don't put it that way.''

''What way?''

''The way that's going to make your brother want to sock me.''

For a few seconds she only stared at him, then her lips swung upward in a full-blown smile. ''You're going to do it!''

''Yes, but only because you're Luke's little sister and you do need to get a little smarter before you go to the city.''

''All right!''

''Right,'' he mumbled, then set his mug in the sink and walked out of the kitchen, into the garage and over to his Mercedes sports car, specifically outlining the terms of his will in his head. Now he wasn't going to be the guy to steal the innocence of Luke Evans's little sister. No. He was going to be the guy who taught her the tricks to attract the guy who would steal her innocence.

He was a dead man.

That fact haunted him enough all day that he avoided Luke like the plague. By the time he arrived home he was a tired, nervous wreck.

Hannah greeted him at the door with Dixon. "Say hello to Daddy."

Jake said, "Hello to Daddy," deciding he might as well make the best of this. Or maybe at least give himself some fun in his last remaining weeks on earth.

Hannah laughed. "You weren't supposed to say that. Dixon was."

"Dixon can't talk."

Hannah turned to the baby she held in her arms. "Dixon?" she coaxed. "Say dad."

The baby grinned toothlessly at her.

"Dixon? Dad. Dad. Dad."

He laughed.

"Dad. Dad. Dad."

Dixon tilted his head.

"Dad. Dad. Dad."

"Ba. Ba. Ba."

Jake felt as if he heart stopped. "My God. He did it. He said dad."

"Not really. He said ba, ba, ba, like a sheep. But he's getting close. I'm guessing 'dad' is going to be his first real word."

With that she turned away, taking his baby to the kitchen. Jake scrambled after them. "Let me hold him."

"Okay. You hold him while I get the macaroni and green beans into serving dishes."

Jake screeched to a halt. "Macaroni and green beans?"

She paused and faced him. "You don't like macaroni?"

"I can't remember the last time I ate macaroni."

"Then this should be a treat for you." She started walking into the kitchen again.

He raced after her. "I hate macaroni!"

"How do you know? You said you can't remember the last time you ate it. Maybe your tastes have changed?"

"Yeah, they've moved up to lobster."

She only smiled. "We'll see."

As it turned out Jake's tastes had not changed and he still considered macaroni to be bland and unappealing. Hannah, however, loved it. Even Dixon seemed to enjoy the tiny nibbles she gave him.

"See. Even Dixon likes it."

"Dixon likes *you*," Jake mumbled because he was having too good a time. Even presented with unappealing food, he was having fun with Hannah.

He tossed his napkin to the table. "I'll take Dixon upstairs for his bath."

"No, we'll both stack the dishes in the dishwasher then we'll both take Dixon upstairs."

"I have a maid," Jake reminded her.

"Yeah, but she only comes in twice a week, and you eat at home now. You didn't before."

"All right. Whatever. If you want to stack the dishes in the dishwasher that's fine. I'll take Dixon upstairs."

She smiled at him. "I'm not sure I trust you alone with him yet."

Jake gaped at her. "Except for visits from my

mother, I was alone with him his entire first weekend here.''

''Yeah, but that was then and this is now.'' She lifted Dixon out of the high chair and nuzzled her nose in his neck. ''He's accustomed to much better care.''

The little boy laughed and grabbed two fistfuls of her hair, bringing her face close so he could press his cheek next to hers in a true gesture of baby affection. Jake's heart swelled before he could stop it. Half of him was jealous that Dixon could be so close to her, could love her, could touch her. The other half was overwhelmed with appreciation for the fact that she loved his child. He didn't think Felicity knew how to love. He knew Amanda, the L.A. nanny, was affectionate, but she hadn't been an overly lovey-dovey woman. But Hannah, even knowing she would only be with Dixon a short time, didn't hesitate to lave love on him.

Almost groaning over the wash of feelings coming over him, Jake stacked the dishes and walked to the swinging door that led to the kitchen. ''Let's just get this over with.''

He put the dishes in the sink to rinse them for the dishwasher and Hannah slid Dixon into his kitchen high chair before she stored the leftover food in the refrigerator.

''I don't think there was really any need to keep the macaroni,'' Jake said as they left the kitchen and headed for the nursery.

Hannah pulled Dixon from his high chair and followed Jake. ''I like it,'' she singsonged. ''And I'll eat it for lunch.''

Dixon laughed, slapping his chubby hands against her cheeks.

"Here, let me take him," Jake said, lifting the little boy from Hannah's arms and arranging him in his own. "You're rambunctious tonight."

Dixon laughed.

"He's been like that all day. I couldn't get him to nap."

"That means he'll sleep well tonight."

"No. With babies, no sleep actually could mean the opposite. The longer he's up, the harder it will be for him to fall asleep."

Jake felt a sense of reprieve slide through him. If they spent all their time tonight caring for Dixon, he might not be forced to teach Love 101. "Which means we'll have to do what?" he asked hopefully.

"Read to him."

"Oh, that's great."

Hannah's eyes narrowed. "You're not still trying to get out of teaching me are you?" she asked as they entered the nursery.

Tired of fighting this, Jake decided to really give her the lessons she desired. After all, she did need to learn how to handle herself. Her naiveté was killing him, and another man might not be so patient. She most definitely could get herself into trouble and Luke really would kill him if he didn't at least teach her something.

He slid Dixon into his play yard, tossed him a toy and turned on Hannah so quickly, she clearly didn't see him coming.

"Sure, I'll teach you," he said, catching her by her elbows and bringing her flush against him. Uncertainty flickered in her eyes, then recognition.

"Are you teaching me how to resist an attack?" she asked happily.

"I *am* an attack."

"Right," she said. Then she giggled. "This is great."

She didn't take him seriously. Not even a little bit. It wasn't that he wanted her afraid. What troubled him was that while she was giggling and enjoying what she considered to be a lesson, he was feeling the unwanted affects of having her slim body pressed against him. He was ten kinds of attracted to her and she was laughing.

"It won't be so great in real life," Jake growled. "For Pete's sake, Hannah, take this seriously."

She sobered instantly. "Okay, I'm serious."

"Great. Fine. Wonderful. You're serious now that I'm out of the mood."

"Oh, so now you're an actor like Dixon's mom. You have to be in the mood to play your part?"

She really didn't get it. And because she didn't get it, she was right. Her naiveté was going to get her into trouble. He turned again, and caught her elbows, but this time he was in no hurry when he brought her flush against him. This time he let his hands slide along her upper arms and down her back. This time he saw her swallow hard before she met his gaze.

And every thought Jake had fell out of his head. She was soft and warm and so pretty he almost couldn't believe she had as little confidence as she had. *He* certainly wanted her. If his situation were different, if he were different, if he could be the man in her life, he wouldn't hesitate to kiss her.

In fact, right now as a part of her lesson he was *supposed* to kiss her. So he did. He let himself bend forward to her upturned face, let his lips brush across hers, feeling her breath pour out on a sigh. Every atom of his body sprang to life and his pulse weakened then sped up again. As his lips brushed over hers, he remembered her innocent response to their kiss the night before, the way she had fallen into it, the way their tongues had mated, and his mind went blank before he crushed her to him. His arms clasped around her shoulders, holding her against him as she melted in his arms. Instincts and feelings Jake had longed for surged to the front of his mind.

Even as they did, he remembered he was supposed to be teaching her, and his heart stopped. If he didn't quickly come up with an excuse for kissing her as though he meant it, she would know he meant it, and they would be back to that awkward place again.

He stepped back and eased away from her, giving the slamming of his heart time to subside by pretending to be examining her response.

"Do you know what you did wrong?"

She stared at him, sleepy-eyed with arousal. "No."

"You didn't even try to control that."

She swallowed.

"You don't just let a man do what he wants," Jake said. "You only let him deepen the kiss and get really intimate if that's what *you* want. If you don't want to kiss like that, you have to stop him, shift your mouth or pull away, because if you don't he's going to think you want to get more intimate, and he'll take it as permission to kiss you any way he wants."

"But what if he's one of the guys I want to kiss?"

"Then you kiss back." At her confused frown he added, "The easiest thing to do is mimic what he does. Think of it like dancing and follow his lead."

Jake stopped when he realized he was teaching her how to kiss. The thought sent a tingle of excitement through him until he reminded himself he was teaching her how to kiss, so another man could enjoy kissing her.

He was, literally, training her for his replacement.

Displeasure snaked through him and he turned away. "Let's just bath Dixon."

She took a quick breath. "Sorry."

He spun to face her. "And stop being sorry!" Anger quickly replaced displeasure. Damn it! Did she have to be so nice? So sweet? So willing to always take the blame.

"Everything is not always your fault!"

Without further explanation, he pushed out of the nursery and bulldozed his way to his office, thinking himself insane to be within ten feet of her when she was off-limits. He slammed the door and marched to his desk where he flopped down on the tall-backed, black leather chair and grabbed the receiver for his phone. From memory he punched in Felicity's cell phone number. One way or another he was ending this. As long as he had Dixon, he needed Hannah. Yet he couldn't live with her. The woman was driving him insane.

So he would do the logical thing. He would call the mother of his child and demand to know when she was returning. At least he would have a deadline so he could count down the days or weeks when he would get his sanity back.

Her cell phone rang five times and suddenly Jake was listening to a recording, directing him to leave a message. He dropped his head to his desk. Fate was trying to kill him.

Or get him killed. He hadn't figured out which yet, but either being around Hannah would just plain kill him or Hannah's brother would do the job once he heard stories of what went on here at Malloy House.

He replaced the receiver of his phone without posting a message and was about to leave his office when his private number rang. The number only one person had.

"Edgar?"

"Yeah, Frank it's me."

"Very funny." Jake frowned.

"It's not meant to be funny. This time tomorrow your name could be Frank."

Jake froze. "What?"

"There's a little part in a black ops assignment that's perfect for a first-timer like you. It's a good way to get you beyond pickups and into a real operation with little to no danger since we haven't yet taught you how to handle that."

Jake's heart skipped a beat. "You're going to train me for dangerous assignments?"

"No. We will teach you how to shoot a gun and a few other rudimentary things. Just not yet. Not until you're sure you want to take the job. And this assignment's a perfect way for you to get a flavor for what you're buying into. The role isn't much. You're actually little more than window dressing."

Jake settled back in his seat as Edgar explained a very tiny part to him. In fact, it was only one step above courier. Still, Jake's salivary glands began to water. This was exactly what he needed to remind himself of all the reasons he couldn't have Hannah Evans. The most important of which was that he liked adventure. In a lot of ways he was just like his dad. And though he hated to admit it, this was the real reason why he had to stay away from Hannah.

"Get my tickets to me and I'll be on the plane," he said, then hung up the phone. He rose from his seat and made his way upstairs again. "Hannah!" he yelled, feeling in control of his life for the first time since she'd arrived. "I just got word I need to take another trip."

Chapter Five

Hannah arrived at the day care the next morning exhausted and grouchy and not anywhere near in the mood to deal with her matchmaking sisters. But to her great delight, when she entered the playroom the only Evans in attendance was Aunt Sadie.

"What's up?" she asked, setting Dixon's travel seat on the counter so she could undo his harness and lift him out.

"Your sisters have gone shopping."

Hannah frowned. "Really?"

"Yes."

Because Sadie's tone was a little odd, Hannah followed her to the filing cabinet beside the computer in the corner of the room that served as her makeshift office.

"You wouldn't have anything to do with this sudden trip, would you?"

"I might have mentioned that your sister Sadie had several planes at her disposal and there were one or two things they still hadn't settled about Caro's wedding. That might have had something to do with them deciding to jet off to New York."

"Oh!" Hannah said through a disappointed sigh. "And they didn't even think to take me?"

"No. Your name came up. In fact, they had all but decided you could leave Dixon here at the day care and go along with them, but I told them no."

Hannah frowned. "Aunt Sadie! This is exactly the kind of stuff I need to be doing! My gosh, I'm such a bumpkin!"

Sadie peered at Hannah over her glasses. "And you think one trip to New York City is going to cure that?"

"No, but…"

"I'm glad you see that. Because I wanted to get you alone today so that I could point out that spending time with Jake Malloy is also not going to magically transform you, Cinderella."

Hannah sighed. "Am I that obvious?"

"No. It took me a few days to figure out what you were doing."

"Great, then Caro, Sadie or Maria should figure it out within the next few minutes."

Sadie laughed. "No. Your sisters are too preoccupied with Caro's wedding and matchmaking you with Jake. I think it will be a while before they see you're just using the poor guy."

Hannah gaped at her aunt. "First of all, the guy isn't poor. Second, I don't think anybody 'uses' Jake."

"That's exactly my point." Sadie took Hannah's free hand and pulled her to the chairs by the desk, nudging her into one seat while she took the other. "Hannah, I've seen the way Jake looks at you, the

same as your sisters have, but while your sisters have
been matchmaking, I've been a little worried.''

"There's nothing to be worried about." Hannah arranged Dixon on her lap. "He was interested, but he
told me he can't be. Two days ago he gave me the
unabridged version of the I-can't-be-interested-in-you
sermon, complete with reasons. He's older than I am.
He doesn't want to settle down. He makes a lousy
boyfriend. I got the abridged version yesterday, and
last night he ran out of the room. Come to think of it,
that's the second time he's run out of the room rather
than finish a discussion... Well, come to think of it,
we hadn't been talking either time." Her face flushed
with embarrassment. "He kissed me. Twice. Then ran
out."

Surprisingly, Sadie smiled. Her face twisted with
confusion as she pondered what Hannah had said, then
she leaned back in her chair and laughed heartily. "He
came right out and told you he can't be interested in
you?"

"Yes."

"Oh, Lord, this is rich. Your sisters are right. He *is*
interested in you."

"I know. He said that," Hannah reminded her aunt.
"But he also said, he can't be."

"Hogwash. The truth is he doesn't know how to
deal with you." Sadie laughed again. "My guess is
you make him feel like settling down and *that* scares
him."

Hannah frowned. Actually, that explained why Jake
constantly tossed references to settling down into their
conversations, though Hannah had never once asked
him to.

Obviously still thinking this through, Sadie narrowed her eyes. "Jake's thirty-three. Whether he knows it or not, he's ready to settle down. Fate dropped his son into his lap, which also dropped a very beautiful, very sweet, very wonderful woman into his household." She laughed unexpectedly. "My guess is our poor Jake is absolutely miserable."

"Well, that makes two of us."

"Ah, so you like him, too."

Hannah stared at her aunt. "Who wouldn't like him?"

"Lots of women. Just like there are lots of men who would look at you and see someone naive and innocent and shrug and move on."

"Thanks for the vote of confidence."

"But Jake hasn't shrugged or moved on."

"No, he's stuck with me because of Dixon."

Sadie shook her head. "He could do a million things with Dixon, including go to an agency in Pittsburgh to hire a real nanny." Sadie took Hannah's hand again. "He isn't getting out because he doesn't want out."

"So what's he doing?"

"Floundering because he doesn't know what to do."

"Great."

"Well, it is great because this opens the door for you to show him what to do."

"Oh, no! No way!" Hannah said emphatically, jumping off the chair and bouncing Dixon in a way that made him giggle. "Every time one of us tries to teach the other anything we end up in trouble!"

"Okay, you either teach him how to settle down or you figure out how to keep your distance," Sadie said, suddenly the disciplinarian Hannah remembered from her teen years. "Because, young lady, you are about to get your heart broken."

Hannah sighed. "I know."

"And that's really why I got rid of your sisters. If you genuinely believe Jake is out of your league, then you need to stop playing games before you get hurt."

She rose, took Hannah by the shoulders and kissed her cheek. "I love you dearly. I like Jake, too. And I think you would make a great couple, but I don't want to see either one of you miserable. So you've got to make a choice one way or the other, either force him to admit he likes you and is ready to settle down or get the heck away from him, because if you don't, you're going to be sorry."

Realizing Aunt Sadie was right, Hannah spent the day with Dixon at the day care, helping Sadie and her parents with the kids and finally making a decision. But in the end she realized there was no decision. Even if she wanted to force Jake to admit his feelings were stronger than his excuses for why he shouldn't have them, she wasn't sophisticated enough to do it. So there could be no relationship between them.

In a sense, fate, environment and her lack of experience made her choice for her. When he returned from his three days in Europe, she would tell him that.

Jake stepped off Troy's Gulf Stream jet at the Sunbright Solutions's landing strip, so happy to be on familiar soil that he could have knelt and kissed the ground.

The small role he had played as Andrea Reese's brother went very, very well, but that was part of the problem. He was so proud of his innate acting talent, his ability to memorize every detail of his role, and the ease with which he carried off the scam of pretending to be Andrea's brother, validating her identity, that he got sloppy. He faltered over his name at a Customs desk because he was daydreaming, telling himself he was right where he was supposed to be, arguing his way out of being attracted to Hannah Evans.

For the first time in his life, thinking about a woman had almost got him arrested. At the very least it had caused Customs to take a closer look at his *fake* passport and scare him witless.

Which only served to reinforce what he had believed all along. He wasn't supposed to like Hannah. Even thinking about her was trouble.

"So, how did it go in Iran?" Troy asked the second Jake stepped into his office that afternoon. "Should we jump on the opportunity to invest in this?"

Jake shrugged. He felt odd about lying to Troy. That was probably because he had never before duped him. Every time Jake went on a courier assignment, he legitimized it by actually investigating an investment. In fact, the investment investigation itself was his cover. This time, he had been working for the CIA. He had been somebody else. He hadn't investigated an investment as a cover. He hadn't used Troy's company money to get his tickets. He hadn't used Troy's plane until he was in Pittsburgh. Troy hadn't foot the bill for Jake's overnight stay. The U.S. government had.

But it was the first time Jake had lied to Troy about his reason for being out of the office, and the lie stuck in his throat. And also reminded Jake that he would have to stop working for Troy if he became a full-time CIA agent.

"I want to do some more investigating," Jake said

and decided that he would find an investment to legitimize that trip.

"Okay. Great," Troy said, then looked at his watch. "I gotta go. It's almost four and the girls have a softball game." He grimaced. "I'm umpiring."

Jake laughed. "They let parents umpire?"

"It's our sworn duty. It's the way they keep everything on the up and up. If anybody wants to yell at today's ump for a bad call all they have to do is remember their day will come behind the plate."

"I'll bet that calms things down considerably."

"Sure does. Hey, why don't you come with us?"

"I can't," Jake said, grinning. "If you're leaving early, so am I. I can't wait to see…"

He almost said Hannah and the baby, but stopped himself. Not only was it a hundred percent wrong to want to see Hannah…but it wasn't right that he put her first! Dear God!

"Dixon," Troy said, then laughed. "Three days away and you forgot your kid's name."

"No. It's jet lag," Jake said, and really believed that was true. It had to be true. He couldn't like Hannah this much. He couldn't have missed her. He couldn't want to see her. It was wrong.

He had himself absolutely convinced he had not missed her. He did not "like" her. And only jet lag caused him to make that mistake, until he walked into his foyer and she stood there holding his son. Dixon looked content and happy perched in her arms, and she looked wonderful. Pretty. Happy. Motherly. The scene made his heart pool in his chest and made his knees weak with longing.

Lord, he was nuts. It was official. He had gone around the bend.

He set his briefcase on the floor and Hannah handed the baby to him. Without hesitating—as if she had read his mind—she said, "Jake, I think you and I need to talk."

"About what?" he asked as he rubbed noses with Dixon. "Hello, little guy." The baby screeched in response and blew spit bubbles.

"A couple of things. First, I was thinking the other day that you should call Dixon when you're away."

He peered over at her. "On the phone?"

"No, I think you should climb to the top of the Alps next time you're in Europe and see if your voice carries... Of course on the phone!"

"He's six months old. He doesn't know how to use the phone."

"I'll put it up to his ear and he'll hear you."

"He won't know it's me."

"He'll recognize your voice."

"Okay, fine. Whatever."

Hannah took a long breath that accentuated her chest and put color in her cheeks, and Jake almost groaned. Why in the name of God did he have to be attracted to her!

"What's the other thing we need to discuss?" he asked, more to get his mind off her chest than to hear her second piece of news.

"Let's go into the family room. We'll put Dixon in the play yard and we'll talk."

"Sounds serious," Jake said, leading the way to the family room, where he deposited Dixon in the play yard and gave him a toy before rising to face Hannah.

"It is serious. It's about us."

His stomach tightened. He couldn't do this. He could not have a conversation where she asked him why he couldn't have a relationship with her. He wasn't sure he would survive if she gave him a dose of those sad eyes and pouty lips that all but melted him into a puddle at her feet. Now that she had had a few days to think about their last kiss, she undoubtedly recognized how attracted he was to her, and optimist that she was, she would insist that meant they should be together because it was clear she was attracted to him.

She inhaled another long breath. "I think I need to be less involved with you, and the best way would be if I stop teaching you how to be a better dad for Dixon. That way we'd spend virtually no time together at all."

Once again, she had found exactly the right way to prick Jake's ego. He felt it deflate and flatten, as he stared at her mutely.

"The single dad school at the day care is really the place where you should be getting your lessons anyway. Caro has classes written specifically with every age group of child in mind. She actually teaches things like discipline, time-out, and how to show your baby you love him."

He stared at her. Now that he was over the prick to his ego, he resented her implication that he needed these lessons. Particularly since he had only set up training sessions with her to offset her need of sophistication lessons from him. "I do show Dixon I love him."

"Yes, you do. You have a lot of natural parenting skills. You have the potential to be a wonderful father and I don't want to screw that up for you."

His eyes narrowed. "How could *you* screw that up?"

She tossed her hands in exasperation. "Because I'm not the best teacher. Caro is."

"Are you sure this isn't more about you not wanting to spend time with me?"

"I just said that!"

"Right," he said, almost stifling a groan because she had basically already admitted all this, yet he was trying to argue her out of it! The entire plane ride from London he had been wondering how to put a wedge between them so they wouldn't always have to fight their attraction all the time. And now that she had done just that, he was arguing against it because it felt like someone had shot him.

Still, he knew she was right. "Okay."

She took the kind of long breath that accentuated her chest and he swallowed hard as she said, "Okay."

From the way he moped during the drive to the day care the next day, Hannah would have thought he was going to the guillotine.

"This won't be that bad, you know."

As if punctuating her statement, Dixon hooted and screeched from his car seat in the back of the SUV.

Jake said, "Right."

"I mean it. You're going to love it," Hannah insisted as he parked the vehicle in the day-care lot and walked around to the back so he could remove Dixon's travel seat.

"Right."

Hannah scampered behind him up to the gate to get them buzzed in. She pressed the button above the lock and announced, "Aunt Sadie, it's me. Hannah. I've brought Jake for his single dad class."

"Nice security," Jake said as the gate buzzed, indicating they could open it. "Did your aunt do this for Troy's twins?"

Hannah shook her head. "No, we've always had this."

"Hmm," Jake said, striding up the walk to the back steps that led to the porch of the two-story house. He carried Dixon, car seat and all, into the big playroom.

Caro saw them first. "Oh, Dixon's here!" She ran over and took the travel seat from Jake's hands. "Hey, Jake. Welcome. I think you're going to like single dad class."

"Right."

"He's not happy," Hannah said. "I think he's afraid of tarnishing his image as a tough guy."

All the Evans sisters laughed. Jake scowled at Hannah. "I'm not worried about my image. I just don't like taking this kind of a bite out of my time when you could just as easily teach me this stuff at home."

"Right," Hannah said, mimicking him as she shook her head and walked away.

Because that was what she was supposed to do. She had to. It was so easy and so much fun to tease him that every second she spent in his company made her like him more. So she had to trade him off to other people, as her aunt Sadie had suggested, before she was in too deep.

But it hurt to watch him tease with Caro. It hurt to see Dixon in Sadie Jr.'s arms. It hurt to be on the outside looking in, and that's what she was. That's what she would always be doing with Jake.

Because there were so many people here to help her aunt, Hannah decided there was no point standing around, feeling out of place and lonely.

"I'm going!" she called to everyone in general and

no one in particular, and stepped out into the hot first-week-of-July sunshine. It felt good to be in fresh air and she inhaled deeply, walking up the street on her way to the diner. She had a sudden urge to be among people. *Her* people. The people she had grown up around. The people she loved and who loved and accepted her just the way she was. The people she would be leaving once she got a job in Pittsburgh. Where, until she made friends, she would also be on the outside looking in. It seemed she just couldn't win.

She pushed open the diner door and the bell rang, announcing her arrival.

"Hey, Hannah!" Charlotte the waitress called from behind the counter. "Find yourself a seat."

"Okay, I'll—" Hannah began but Jake's mother stopped her.

"Sit with us, Hannah," she called, waving to the booth she shared with her new husband, Larry.

Though Hannah wasn't sure it was a good idea to sit with Jake's mom, she realized they would probably talk more about Dixon than anything else. And that was a good idea because it would be a tidy reminder that she was Dixon's nanny, nothing more, and that she needed to get over her feelings of possessiveness for both the baby and his daddy.

She walked to the booth, smiling at Jake's mother. With her dark hair and dark eyes, Georgiann Malloy was still as gorgeous as she had been in Hannah's first memories when she was young. Georgiann's new husband, an investment counselor who'd moved to Wilburn from Pittsburgh and now commuted to work three days a week, rose as Hannah approached.

"I'll just scoot across the table with my woman," he said, sliding off his seat and over to sit with Georgiann. Tall and muscular, with thinning brown hair and a perfect smile, Larry was a nice match for Georgiann.

"Are you having breakfast?" Charlotte asked cheerfully as she approached the table.

"No. Just get me coffee. I'm trying to kill some time until I'm needed again."

"Will do!" Charlotte said, sliding her pencil behind her ear and scurrying away.

Georgiann leaned forward conspiratorially. "I heard you banished Jake to single dad school."

Hannah laughed at the phraseology. "I tried teaching him myself. It didn't work out."

Larry glanced at his watch. "Speaking of work! I better get home and make some calls. Don't forget to tell Hannah to tell Jake we're taking Dixon to Idlewild on Saturday for Grandparents Day." He quickly kissed Georgiann and rose from the booth. "See you later, Hannah," he said, then left.

"He's such a nice guy."

Georgiann's eyes glowed. "He's a wonderful guy."

"How did you meet him?"

"Through Jake, believe it or not. He decided to have a party on the *Gateway Clipper* and invited everybody from Pittsburgh he knew, even if he'd only met them once, just to fill up the boat."

Hannah laughed musically. "Jake knows how to have fun."

"Yeah, he does," Georgiann agreed, but she sighed. "I just wish he'd find a good woman to have that fun with and settle down."

Hannah played with the roll of silverware Charlotte had left behind for her. "I don't think that's going to happen. Your son seems really, really happy as a single person."

"I know. And now that he has an heir there's no reason for him to marry. I might as well forget about being mother of the groom."

Trying to lighten the mood, Hannah said, "You might not get a wedding, but at least you got a grandchild."

"Yes. I guess have to accept that I have a very unusual son with a very unusual life."

"Is that so bad?"

"It wouldn't be if I felt this was what he wanted and didn't feel like I'm to blame for the fact that he lives like this."

Hannah gaped at Georgiann. In spite of being divorced, then having her ex-husband die, meaning she didn't even get child support, she had raised Jake well. She had been an exceptional parent. Going to every football game, cheering her heart out, selling chances for football boosters.

"How can you blame yourself?"

Georgiann shrugged. "I think I should have remarried sooner."

Hannah frowned. "I don't see how that had any bearing on things."

"For starters, staying single while I raised Jake was like saying that I didn't need to be married. I started off with good intentions. I didn't want to saddle another man with Jake's care." She paused to grin. "I also didn't care for anybody else's opinion or influence on how I was raising him."

Understanding that kind of stubborn streak, Hannah laughed. "Makes sense to me."

"Yeah, but it was a sacrifice. I gave up having a

relationship. I gave up companionship. I made it look like so much fun, I don't think Jake realized I was sacrificing and I think I might have taught him it's good to be alone.''

"Oh.''

"Yeah, oh. And even if you don't look at it that way, the other side of the coin is that I didn't give him a very good example. I didn't show him how to settle down, how to be married. Jake has no blueprint for how to be in a stable relationship.''

Hannah said nothing, but remembered her aunt Sadie had mentioned something similar when they'd had their big talk the day before. That Jake was scared because he didn't know what to do. She had even suggested Hannah could teach Jake.

"You, on the other hand, had a great example in your parents. And if your parents weren't enough, all you have to do is look at your sisters. My goodness, talk about marrying well. Both settled down two men who were determined to stay single! Just watching them should have taught you everything you need to know about falling in love and starting a new life with someone.'' She laughed. "If you've been paying any attention at all, you could write a manual.''

"I couldn't…''

"Sure you could. Think this through, Hannah. Even if you were too young when Maria got married, you saw Caro and Sadie Jr. fall in love. Just stop and think objectively about everything your two sisters did and you will probably easily see the steps they took along the way.''

Rising from the booth, Georgiann laughed. "You need to write the book! There are millions of kids from single parent families coming into maturity right now and you could get rich!''

Hannah didn't think Georgiann's idea would make her rich, but Georgiann had made her very solidly doubt the decision about Jake she had made the day before. She never once considered looking to her sisters for an example of what to do. She was too busy trying to stay out of their matchmaking ways to see that their romances were the example she should be studying to figure out this situation with Jake. After all, Max wasn't the kind of guy anybody thought would settle down, either. And Troy hadn't wanted to settle down again. He had been married before. He had his children and his company to give his life meaning. But Sadie had convinced him to fall in love one more time, and Hannah had watched her do it. If she really stopped to remember the details of the romance of either of her sisters, she could easily figure out what to do with Jake.

But Georgiann's advice had come one day too late. The dye had been cast. Jake was enrolled in single dad school. And they no longer had any reason to even communicate, let alone spend big chunks of time together.

Chapter Six

That night when she went to bed, Hannah tossed and turned, miserable that she had ruined everything.

She had never met anybody like Jake Malloy and she suspected she might never meet anybody like him again. He was sophisticated, good-looking, charming, interesting, well-traveled, intelligent and it didn't hurt that he was rich. She hadn't been surprised to melt when he kissed her. She hadn't been surprised to be blown away by his looks, personality and charm. Any woman would be. What surprised her, unnerved her, was the sense of rightness she felt in his house, in his arms. And the sense of loneliness she had had that morning as he attended single dad class without her.

She punched her pillow and tried again in vain to fall asleep, but the thoughts kept coming. When she cared for Dixon, she didn't feel like a custodian or guardian for a child. Nurturing instincts rose up in her and caused her to feel love and affection for Jake's little boy as if the baby were her own. When she made dinners, terrible though they were, she wasn't simply putting food on the table. She was caring for the people in her life. She didn't feel like a stranger or interloper in the kitchen, the bathroom or even this bedroom. She didn't even have the sense of staying in a hotel. Nope. Oddly enough, she felt as though she was home. She was exactly where she was supposed to be.

Except when she kissed Jake, Hannah amended in her thoughts. Then she didn't feel as if she was supposed to be in this bedroom. She had the uncanny, indescribably achy feeling that she was supposed to be in his. And if he really was fighting an equal attraction to her, or confused about the affection growing between them, then wasn't she a fool to have thrown away any chance she might have with him?

Yeah, she was a fool because she had thrown it away. She punched her pillow one more time. And there wasn't a damn thing she could do about it. She was stuck with this decision that she had made too hastily. Yet another proof that she could really use the sophistication lessons he had been giving her and probably would still be giving her, except that she had broken their deal.

Or had she?

The truth was, she hadn't said she didn't want any more lessons from him. She had simply told him he needed to go to single dad school. She hadn't said she no longer wanted *her* lessons.

That conclusion made her sit up in bed because it was true. She knew she wouldn't marry Jake. She had no ability to seduce him into admitting he liked her. She wasn't really sophisticated enough to get him to settle down. She wasn't going to pretend she had a hope in hell of even getting him to kiss her again. But there was at least a slim thread of possibility that she could get him to resume teaching her.

The next morning Jake stared at Hannah incredulously as she puttered around the kitchen, doing things that didn't really need to be done. What she had just proposed was absolutely insane and Jake suspected she didn't have the nerve to look at him.

"So what you're saying is that you're going to hold me to my promise to give you sophistication lessons, even though you reneged on your promise to help me with Dixon by handing me off to the single dad school."

"I suppose you could say that," Hannah agreed, and Jake noticed again that she wouldn't look at him.

"I'm definitely saying that," he argued, but Hannah didn't reply. Instead she kept puttering around the kitchen as if his teaching her was a done deal.

Jake sighed. Just standing in the same room with her, hearing her melodious voice, seeing her pretty smile, he was having those "wrong" feelings about her again. He didn't think it was wise to return them to that kind of close proximity. He certainly wouldn't be providing any more instructions on kissing.

Unfortunately he couldn't explain that to Hannah without admitting his unholy attraction to her, which would only get him in trouble, so he grabbed the best excuse he could find.

"Hannah, even if I did agree that I should continue teaching you, our time is limited because I need to be with Dixon. Especially today. Saturday is the only full day I have with him."

She shrugged. "Sorry, but I saw your mother and Larry at the diner yesterday. They're taking the baby.

Something about a grandparents day at Idlewild Park.''

"Great.''

"See, you don't even have a real reason not to keep up your end of the bargain.''

He had plenty of reasons and right now most of them were centered in his groin. In her sedate little blouse and pretty capri pants she looked carefree and cuddly, so tempting that he was dying.

She was so different from the other women he dated that he couldn't believe how much he wanted her...

Wait a minute.

Maybe that was the point? Maybe he found her attractive because she was so different from every other woman in his life? Maybe if she looked like every other woman he dated, he wouldn't want her anymore? That made very good sense. Plus, by asking him to help her, she had actually given him the venue to turn her into a woman just like all the others who didn't tempt him.

Oh, this was brilliant!

"Hannah, you're right. I should keep up my end of the bargain. But you have to promise to put yourself completely in my hands.''

He could see from the way her eyes widened then narrowed that she'd taken all the wrong meanings from that. He knew it when she frowned.

Good, let her be off center for a change. It finally dawned on him that this woman, who was supposed to be innocent, certainly wasn't intimidated by him and frequently got the better of him.

Well, this time he was winning.

"Completely in my hands or no deal.'' He shoved out his hand to shake hers. "I mean it.''

Cautious, eyes still narrowed and focused on his face, she took his hand. Trying to behave as innocently as she did, Jake shook once. When the expected jolt of electricity zapped up his arm, he ignored it. He was getting her out of his system once and for all today.

After his mother and stepfather picked up the baby, Jake drove Hannah to Somerset, Pennsylvania. Though the tiny town was a very unlikely place to find one of the best hairdressers in the United States, Somerset was Anton Novelli's home. Though Anton did most of his work in New York City, he spent summers and weekends hiding in his old hometown. Felicity had found him by accident, stumbling across him at a party she attended while staying at Jake's house. Once she realized he was the same Anton Novelli who was one of New York's most sought-after stylists and makeover artists, keeping her beautiful was his payment for her to keep the location of his weekend retreat a secret.

"Hmm," Anton said, walking around Hannah as if she were a science experiment. Hannah graced Jake with a worried look. He only smiled.

"Hannah is Dixon's nanny," Jake said, explaining the situation to the man he hoped would make Hannah totally unappealing to him by making her look just like Felicity. "She's a schoolteacher, who lost her job, so she's planning to leave for Pittsburgh as soon as Felicity gets back from her movie shoot."

Anton's black eyebrows rose and he stopped pondering Hannah to gape at Jake. "Felicity got a movie?"

Jake laughed. "She's not that bad of an actress."

"No, she's not. For months she had you totally convinced she was lovable."

Jake scowled.

Hannah said, "Really?"

"Yeah, really," Anton said conspiratorially. "When Felicity got pregnant our Jake wanted to do the right thing, but Felicity refused. Said they wouldn't be good married to each other. She said she couldn't trust herself to be faithful any more than she could trust Jake to be loyal to her. They were the talk of the 'set.'"

"What set?" Hannah asked.

"Yeah, what set?" Jake echoed.

"You know. The crowd. The set. Our peeps."

Jake frowned. "Our peeps?"

Anton laughed. "Our people. Peeps," he said, then laughed again. "Jake, you gotta get up to the city more."

"Jake's out of town enough," Hannah said as Anton directed her to a chair. "Dixon shouldn't be without one or the other of his parents and since Jake is the guardian right now, I think he should stay home more."

"Tell me about Dixon." Anton looped a cape around Hannah, then pulled her long yellow hair from beneath it before he turned his attention to her reflection in the mirror to survey her hair and face.

"He's adorable."

"Does he look like Mommy or Daddy?"

"Mommy."

"Oh, yum. For all her faults Felicity is gorgeous."

Jake leaned against the doorjamb of the room off the kitchen of Anton's summer home that had been converted into a mini beauty shop for just this kind of emergency. Listening to Hannah and Anton discuss Felicity, Jake held back a snicker. The more they talked about Jake's old girlfriend and the fact that Jake had almost married her, the better, because Anton was as much a matchmaker as Hannah's sisters. Now that he had made the connection of Jake almost marrying Felicity, it was a sure bet he would make Hannah look like her.

Anton glanced up. "I thought you were leaving?"

"Nope. I'm staying here to make sure you do this right."

The beautician struck the offended artist pose. "Not hardly."

"Anton, I'm the one paying. That means I stay."

"Then I'll do it for free. Scat."

"No."

He reached for Hannah's cape. "Okay, then no haircut at all. Shame, too. I was going to make her beautiful."

Jake sighed. Anton would make her beautiful and though Jake wanted her beautiful in the sophisticated-fashion-model way that would make her resistible, he was also doing this for Hannah. She genuinely wanted a fair shake in Pittsburgh and Jake knew appearances were everything. Especially first impressions. Plus, he had promised Hannah he would help her. Even if she had reneged on her end of the deal by sending him to the single dad school, and though he had argued about this over breakfast, he believed he should keep his promise. Not for his integrity, but for her. Because he liked her. In spite of their odd dealings, odd feelings, and sexual attraction that was bound to get him in trouble, he liked her and he wanted this for her.

"I'll only leave if you promise not to gossip," he

said, assuring that Anton would gossip if only because he didn't like to be told what to do. But that was what Jake wanted. He wanted Anton focused on Felicity and making Hannah look as sophisticated as Felicity. Since that was what Hannah had said she wanted.

"I promise not to gossip."

Jake made a pained noise, as if he recognized Anton would gossip anyway, but he left.

Hannah turned to Anton. "And here I was hoping to get all the good dirt."

"Oh, you will. I never consider the truth gossip. I see myself more as a newspaper."

Hannah laughed.

"What do you want to know?"

"Everything."

Anton lifted Hannah's golden tresses. "I'm guessing that's because you like Jake as more than an employer."

As far as Hannah was concerned, this issue had been laid to rest last night and she wasn't going back. "No. I'm just curious. He seems to have led an interesting life."

Anton stared at her. "You haven't come to me for good hair to make you attractive to him and good gossip to assure you don't make the same mistakes other women have made?"

Hannah frowned. Was it her imagination, or was everybody in the world trying to marry off Jake Malloy? And why did everybody automatically assume she would want to be the one to settle down with him? Did she and Jake give off some kind of scent or signal that said, "Marry us off"? Whatever the case, Hannah was beginning to understand why Jake balked every time anybody mentioned it and she felt the sudden urge to protect him.

"Nope. It's not like that with Jake and me. If we seem closer than the usual nanny/employer it's because I'm the baby sister of his best friend. He's nine years older than I am and I'm a hundred years less sophisticated than he is. I don't want him any more than he wants me."

Anton smiled congenially. "Okay. I get it. You need to be beautiful. He's trying to help. There are a hundred styles we could pick from for you. Luckily I can choose any of them because you have long hair."

She *did* have long hair, Hannah thought, her heart racing and her limbs numb with fear as she watched Anton chop off inch after beautiful inch. First he convinced her to donate her golden tresses to Locks of Love, and he took the first foot in one long bite, carefully saving every gorgeous yellow strand to be woven into wigs for children who had lost their hair due to illness. Then he began snipping.

She would have cried. She would have sobbed, actually, because she had never had short hair in her life, but she kept telling herself this haircut was for two good causes. Not just her own poise and self-confidence, but also for sick children. But when Anton turned her to face the mirror and she saw the mature woman staring back at her, all her doubts about liking short hair slipped away and her mouth fell open.

"Kind of amazing, isn't it?" Anton said, standing back to gloat over her.

"Oh, my God."

"Such a pretty face to be hidden by all that hair."

Hannah only stared.

"Men supposedly like long hair better, but some women are much more attractive with short." He paused, caught her gaze and added, "Are you sure you don't like Jake? Because with this look you're going to knock his socks off."

She fingered her pretty new locks, then swallowed hard. "I'm sure."

"Okay," Anton said and began to do her makeup. "But I think that's a big mistake. The man is so ready to settle down he looks like he could explode."

Hannah resolutely shook her head. "I'm sure."

Just as Anton had finished explaining Hannah's new cosmetics to her, they heard the crunch of gravel of a car pulling into Anton's driveway. Anton ran to the window to see who it was.

"He's here. That means you've got about thirty seconds." He turned her to face the mirror again. "Take a good look at the entirely new you and reconsider. Are you going to take this new look and run with it, or are you going to wimp out on me?"

Jake called, "I'm back," as he walked toward Anton's provisional salon. He took a long breath, prepared to see that Anton had made Hannah a miniature version of Felicity, then pulled away the curtain, just as Hannah turned to face the doorway. When he saw that Anton hadn't poofed and curled her hair like Felicity's, he almost gasped. Not because her hair was different from what he expected—short and sleek, stopping just at her chin. But because the hairdo made her look absolutely gorgeous. And older. She no longer looked like a girl on the verge of womanhood. She looked like a woman. She *was* a woman.

He felt as if someone had punched him in the stomach.

Hannah said, "Now, my clothes are all wrong. Jake, take me shopping?" She turned those big green eyes on him, eyes made more beautiful, more vivid and more sensual by the fact that there was no hair to distract them from view. "I've got money budgeted to buy some new things for interviewing and working in Pittsburgh and I have my bank card," she said, waving it. "So please?"

"Sure," he said, then internally cursed himself. He hadn't even hesitated a second. Nope. He jumped to do what she wanted. Which was probably why Anton was smirking.

Jake tried to take Hannah to the outlet malls nearby, but she insisted on going to one of the Pittsburgh area malls. The one-hour drive was punctuated by her happy chatter and expressions of delight over how much older she looked, and Jake couldn't have agreed more. In fact, what he wanted to do was to stop the car, grab her and kiss that happy mouth, because seeing her so filled with joy, filled him with joy…and ridiculously aroused him. Which only reinforced that his plan was backfiring and he needed to make a new one.

"How else am I going to get clothes like the clothes the women in Pittsburgh are wearing if I don't shop in Pittsburgh?" she asked as she led him to the mall's front entrance.

He didn't say anything as he opened the door for her. In his head he was planning his new strategy. Anton had failed him. He'd expected him to give Hannah a hairdo like Felicity's. He hadn't. Jake had also expected Hannah to be a little off center with her new hair, maybe shy, maybe looking for approval. Instead she was so pleased she couldn't stop chattering. So confident, she wasn't asking for things anymore, she was telling him what they would do.

And he was following because he had no plan. Damn it. *Think!* he commanded himself. Think!

His gaze wandered over to Hannah. To her happy face, her gorgeous new hairdo, the once-pouty mouth that seemed to be in a permanent grin.

He couldn't remember why he wanted her out of his life.

Hannah immediately led him to Kauffman's. They walked past the posters advertising the bridal division and Jake's steps faltered. *This* was why he wanted her out of his life. She was the kind of woman a man settled down with and he wasn't the settling-down kind. No. That wasn't entirely correct. The truth was exactly the opposite. He wasn't the kind of man a smart woman would want to settle down with. As a kid given too many choices because he was a star football player in a small town, Jake had more than misspent his youth and beyond. He would come to a marriage with lots of women in his past, and no sane woman would gamble her future on the hope that Jake could actually settle down.

Hannah would figure that out the same way Felicity had and, when she did, she would dump him and things would be awkward for everybody in her family and his family for years to come.

So, no. He couldn't go any further than he already had with Hannah. He had made the decision not to be a one-woman man almost two decades ago when he realized it hadn't worked for his father, so it probably wouldn't work for him, either, and it was too late to turn back or to even change his mind. There was no point pretending he could, or that his past didn't matter, because it did matter for someone like Hannah.

"Hannah, nothing is ever going to come of you and me. I'm not the kind of person to get married. Through my bad behavior, I made that choice almost twenty years ago and I can't change it now. Even Felicity wouldn't marry me when she got pregnant because she knew who I was," he said, looking into those sexy green eyes and finally understanding something he had missed until this moment. With her hair cut short and makeup on, she didn't have an air of innocence anymore. That caused him to really think about how she had behaved with him over the past few weeks, and he realized she might be a tad naive, but she wasn't stupid. In fact, she was pretty damned smart. And he decided it was time he and everybody else in her life stopped treating her like a baby.

"But that doesn't mean we can't shop together," he added, leading her to his favorite department— sportswear. He still couldn't have a relationship with her, but at least he wasn't going to worry about her anymore. She no longer looked like someone so gullible and innocent that unscrupulous men would see her as an easy mark. In fact, in more stylish clothes she might actually be able to intimidate disreputable men away from her.

Hannah watched as Jake stopped at a row of cute cut-off jeans, beside a display of denim mini-skirts. For a good twenty seconds she studied his wonderful profile, the shapes and angles that made up his too handsome face, and knew exactly why he had felt the need to tell her yet again that he wasn't the kind of person to get married. This time it wasn't something she had done. Nope. He assumed Anton had tried to play matchmaker and he wanted to make sure nothing Anton said had stuck. But this time the reminder didn't feel like an insult. Now that she agreed with Jake that they didn't have a future together, clearing the air made her feel as if a weight had been lifted off her shoulders and that they really were free to just shop.

Nothing on her mind but getting some new clothes and having some fun with a very interesting guy, who probably had forgotten more about having a good time than she would ever learn, she picked up a miniskirt.

"What do you think of this?"

"I think they won't let you wear it to class."

"I don't think you brought me here to buy new things for school. Besides, I'm suddenly in the mood for some new casual clothes. Some new clothes to wear this summer while I care for your son... Hey! Don't you have a pool?"

She had already snagged a red halter top, denim miniskirt and two pairs of the cut-off jean shorts, so as she said the last she headed for the bathing suits. She liked the tank suits. She liked the two-piece suits with the tap pants bottoms. But she never had a string bikini. She'd never even worn a thong. She grabbed one of the thong bikinis.

"Oh, look at this!"

Jake looked, and when he saw the three scraps— and he did mean scraps—of material being held by the baby sister of his best friend, he swallowed hard. Though he had pronounced immature Hannah gone for good and decided she could hold her own with most men, he hadn't factored a bikini into the mix. And no matter how much he intended to treat her maturely, he couldn't forget this was Luke's little sister and that he had some responsibility to his friend.

"You don't need that suit."

"Of course, I don't need it. I want it. You have a pool. And I've never worn one of these before." She ticked the things off on her fingers before dangling the bikini and smiling at him. "I wonder what it's like to swim in bottoms that are little more than dental floss? I bet it would be like swimming naked."

Jake almost choked. Not so much because of what she said, but because it brought him a vivid image of her in his pool, the cool water sliding over her naked curves. And though he wouldn't mind coming home to that, he knew Luke would kill him.

He grabbed the suit and tucked it back on the rack. "It's not for you."

She took it out again. "I think it is." She laughed. "Come on, Jake, I'll only wear it when I'm by myself. Your pool has a fence. Besides, your house is out in the country. It's not like anybody's going to know I'm there or what I'm doing."

He would know she was there and what she was doing. Every afternoon, while his son napped, Jake would be thinking about her sunbathing nearly naked, or blissfully slithering through the water of his pool. With her new hair and new personality and easy acceptance of the fact that a permanent relationship wasn't on the table, Jake began to feel as though they could have his usual kind of relationship. One that could be satisfying without leading to marriage.

But he knew Luke would kill him for that, too.

Without another word, she marched toward the dressing room. Jake sat—collapsed, really—on the chair beside the door and scrubbed his hand over his face. Felicity had finally phoned and told him her movie would last three months. If he didn't soon get ahold of himself, he was going to snap and do something he would regret for the rest of his life.

Mercifully, Hannah didn't try on the bathing suit…or if she did, she didn't model it. She did, however, model the miniskirt and red halter top. When she emerged from the curtained dressing room and a long length of her leg was at his eye level, his mouth went dry.

"What do you think?"

He peeled his eyes away from her legs, not letting them ride up her curves but forcing them to immediately catch her gaze. "I think no self-respecting teacher would wear that around Wilburn."

She turned to look at herself in the full-length mirror and smiled. "Where would she wear it?"

His attention fixed on her happy face, her eyes lit with joy, her mouth curved into a permanent smile, he could think of a hundred places she could wear this outfit. He could think of cities and towns with open-minded people who would welcome her with open arms. Beaches. Clubs. All places he suddenly wanted to show her because he knew she had never been anywhere and showing her things would be like seeing them for the first time himself.

He felt the shiver of danger again. The shiver that meant he was crossing the line from physical attraction to genuine affection, and though he easily hid it from Hannah, he couldn't hide it from himself. He wanted to show her the world and everything in it. He wanted to share things with her, teach her things, be there when she woke up in Paris. And if he didn't stop these feelings, he was the one who was going to get hurt, because he was starting to want things he couldn't have.

"Hannah, you could wear it anywhere you want," he said, careful to sound objective and impersonal, not mean-spirited or distant. They had to live together until Felicity came for Dixon and they could only do that as long as they behaved.

He glanced at his watch. "And it's also close to one. Buy that outfit, we'll grab lunch and then we'll head for the teacher clothes. I'm guessing you probably do need a new interview suit."

She bought four new suits, three skirts, three flattering tops to go with the skirts, and more stylish casual clothes than Jake thought could fit into the trunk of his sports car.

"Squish them," she said, happily shoving shopping bags into the trunk before he slammed it shut. "I don't care."

Jake laughed in spite of himself. "You're certainly having fun today."

"Yes," she said as he pulled out into traffic. Because he had the top down on his convertible, the wind caught her hair and made the short, silky strands ripple.

Jake ignored the physical reaction he automatically had to reach out and caress her hair. So, he liked her. Who wouldn't? She was a sweet, likable person. And now she wasn't simply a beautiful woman. She was a beautiful woman experiencing and appreciating her beauty for the first time. She was nearly irresistible but he had to control himself. He was the older, stronger, smarter one.

Unfortunately, the more maturely she behaved, the

more he wondered if she really would be hurt by an affair. The truth was, she might see it as part of what she needed to learn for her life in the big city. And if he didn't delve into that lesson, he would be sending her off ill-prepared.

That thought nagged him when he switched from the convertible to his SUV to pick up his son. He thought about it as Dixon yelped and screeched from his car seat in the back. He thought about it as he and Hannah bathed Dixon and put him to bed. He thought about it when he met her in the downstairs foyer, right before she put her foot on the bottom step to go to her room for the night.

"No cocoa tonight?" he asked.

She shook her head. "I'm not in a cocoa mood."

Of course not. Nothing would be as it had been for her anymore. With her confidence soaring, she had laid aside all girlish things and stepped into the role of woman.

His voice sounded scratchy and rough when he said, "No, I didn't think you were."

She looked up and caught his gaze. "Thanks for all this. I know we had more than a few miscommunications that were uncomfortable for you. I'm glad you stuck with me."

He said, "I'm glad I did, too," and almost touched her hair, but he stopped himself because he wasn't sure of anything right now and he didn't want to make a mistake that could potentially hurt Hannah if he was misinterpreting her. His dad couldn't keep his hands off all the wrong women, and that had led to a divorce and continuing gossip that always hurt his mother. When Jake became a small-town hero, presented with opportunities for women and fun most kids didn't have, he saw the traits of his father in himself and rationalized that as long as he never hurt anyone, he wasn't a ''bad'' guy. So he was always honest with the girls he dated about what he wanted—and didn't want.

But the funny part of it was, he didn't think Hannah was the one who would get hurt in this situation. He had a sneaking suspicion that if any woman could turn the tables on him, it would be Hannah. If he stayed too long with her, or went too far, she would be the one who would hurt him.

But that didn't stop him from longing to kiss her. For a good ten seconds they gazed into each other's eyes. When he saw the color of her eyes darken then glisten with the same desire he had in his gut, he knew that if he kissed her now it would be like kissing a new person. He wouldn't have to teach her anything. She would instinctively know exactly how to please him. In fact, he wouldn't be surprised if she kissed him first, her confidence had grown that much.

But instead of kissing him, she took a pace back. ''Good night, Jake,'' she said, then hurried up the steps.

Chapter Seven

The next morning Jake scrambled to the NannyCam. His number one priority all along had been not to hurt Hannah, not to lead her on, yet he kept doing foolish things. Even though he hadn't kissed her the night before, he had wanted to, desperately, and he knew that she had recognized that. So she had been the one to turn away.

He fell onto his chair and flipped on his computer screen. She might have seemed perfectly calm and in control when she turned and raced up the steps. Hell, she might have *been* calm and in control. But that didn't mean she had stayed calm. She could have had all kinds of second thoughts before drifting off to sleep. If that almost-kiss had caused her to mistrust him, she could be rethinking all the changes she had made. She might even want him to take her to Pittsburgh to return all the clothes she had bought. And that would be a tragedy because she looked great in those outfits, and she needed the confidence they gave her for her new job in a bigger, more sophisticated environment.

Using his mouse, he tapped the icon to bring the nursery on-screen and there stood Hannah, dressed in her new short-shorts, her cropped hair bouncing as she blew on Dixon's belly. Not only was she happy, apparently unaffected by what had almost happened between them the night before, but also she was wearing the clothes. She hadn't changed her mind. She looked fabulous and comfortable, perfectly content and at home with her new look.

His stomach tightened. Her transformation was permanent. And though that was good since she would be moving away, he suddenly realized that also meant he was going to have to live with this happy, sexy woman, without touching her—without even looking as if he wanted to touch her. That thought made him want to punch Luke.

"We're only giving your daddy one more minute, Dixon, then we're bathing you without him."

Jake tilted his head in question, unable to figure out why she was expecting him to join her. She was the one who had sent him to single dad school, telling him she wasn't going to teach him anymore.

"Your daddy loves you," she cooed, again tickling Dixon's tummy. "And pretty soon he's going to get to the point where you're the first thing he wants to see in the morning."

Jake frowned. Actually, that was part of why he ran to the NannyCam. He wanted to see Hannah, gauge her mood, give himself time to figure out what to do, but he also loved seeing Dixon. He loved seeing Hannah play with Dixon.

"I think a few more lessons at the day-care center and your dad's going to be the best dad in the world."

Surprised by the compliment, since he pretty much figured she should think he was slime for almost kissing her when he kept saying he didn't want a relationship with her, Jake sat back in his chair and his chest puffed out with pride. He *was* a good dad, if only because he loved Dixon. He loved that little boy so much he had been willing to learn how to mix formula, make bottles, buy baby food…and change diapers. He certainly didn't do them correctly all the time. He certainly did do them all well. But he always gave anything that had to do with his son his best shot.

"I think that once your dad learns that he can be a little messy with you, he's going to want to spend more time with you."

Jake frowned again. Though Jake disliked diapers, Dixon's messiness wasn't why he didn't spend a lot of time with his son. Jake was simply too busy. Most days he couldn't come home from work any earlier than he did. When he was out of town, he frequently didn't return to his hotel until late into the night.

"I think when he goes away on his trips, he sort of loses his connection to you and when he returns it's almost like starting over again with you for him."

Jake tapped his pencil on his desk, wondering if this was why she had suggested he call Dixon when he was away. Not so much for the baby, but to remind himself that he had a child. If she had, she was brilliant, because he did sometimes forget he was a dad when he was away. Not because he didn't love or miss his son, but because he got caught up in other things. Then when he got home, he instantly had to become a different person. Or maybe three different people. A vice president for Troy since he now also worked for Sunbright Solutions in addition to being Troy's investment partner, a boss for the employees he supervised and a dad for Dixon.

Dixon cooed at Hannah and Hannah made a funny noise and nuzzled his neck. "I'm not sure how we'll teach him to always think of himself as your dad, to stop forgetting about you completely when he's away, but I think keeping him actively involved is a good start."

Jake sat a little farther back in his chair. Her insights amazed him until he realized he shouldn't be surprised that the person caring for his son was the one who could most clearly see his parental shortcomings. But hearing his problem so succinctly stated gave Jake an odd feeling in the pit of his stomach. Hannah was correct when she said that every time he went on a trip he had trouble getting back into the swing of things at home. Especially this last time. Because he had been on the CIA assignment, pretending to be someone else, he had forgotten all about Troy, Sunbright Solutions, any investment he might be considering for himself and Troy…and Dixon. He would be lying if he didn't admit he had forgotten he had a son. He would be kidding himself if he didn't recognize the problem would get worse once Felicity took his son back to L.A.

He pondered that as Hannah made funny faces and odd noises that entertained his baby. He studied her tempting mouth and watched her pretty hair bounce, and realized she was a perfect combination of sex appeal to satisfy his male instincts and sweetness necessary to raise children, along with intelligence to listen to him, talk to him, be his partner and confidante.

She wasn't the first woman in his life to have all three, but she was the first woman to have them in a way or an amount that caught his attention and held it. Though he had asked Felicity to marry him, Hannah was the first woman he could actually envision as his wife.

He knew it was wrong to let his thoughts roam, but he couldn't help it. Filled with an unexpected longing over something he wanted but couldn't have, he wondered what it would be like to be her husband, to know someone sweet and lovable waited for him each night, to know she cared for his children—cared for *him*— to know she would love him unconditionally.

His eyes fixed on the image on the computer screen, and he experienced an unexpected warmth and a peace. The kind of peace he had always suspected existed, but had never known growing up in a hectic single-parent home, with a dad who had been the talk of the town until he died when Jake was twelve. But even as Jake absorbed the feeling of tranquility, he reminded himself he couldn't have it. His course had been set long ago. He wouldn't get married. Hannah wouldn't be his wife.

Pain squeezed his heart, but Dixon moved, causing Jake's focus to shift to his son, and he came to an astounding realization. He couldn't have Hannah. That wasn't so much a choice as a reality. But Dixon was a reality, too. As much his "family" as any potential wife would be.

Suddenly, Jake felt as if he was shirking his responsibility. Having had Dixon in his custody had taught him being a dad meant more than being a source for money and the sometimes visitor he had been since Dixon's birth. The commitment he needed to make to his son even went beyond bottles and feeding and changing diapers. The love of a parent for a child should be all-encompassing. He had to "be there" more for Dixon.

Of course, he wouldn't always be able to "be there" since Felicity had the baby most of the time, and Jake having him for long periods would be few and far between. But that only made it more obvious to Jake that he wasn't making the most of the time he had with his son.

And he also sensed that was what Hannah was saying. What she had been saying all along.

He brought his gaze back to the screen just as Hannah picked up the bear with the NannyCam in its eyes. His own eyes widened, his mouth fell open and he almost yelled "No!" But he realized she wouldn't hear him anyway.

She took the bear and waved it in Dixon's face. Jake knew this because he got a sudden full-screen rocking vision of the round eyes, pudgy nose and spit-bubble lips of his giggling son. Then the scene became blurred and ruffled as she swept the bear away from Dixon. The camera was suspended chest level, and considering that Hannah was wearing one of her new, trendier and also lower-cut shirts, Jake got a very clear shot of her cleavage. Then, with the speed of light, the bear began to move toward her chest. She buried the bear's nose in her bosom and Jake got a twelve-inch screen full of creamy white breast.

His breath caught. His throat tightened. Other parts of his anatomy sprang to life.

Before he could do more than gasp, Hannah pulled the bear away, tickled it in Dixon's face, then punched it against her breasts.

Jake began to choke again because with the introduction of something so personal into the film, he really was spying. *Spying!* Though the CIA was currently recruiting him, he didn't think the first person he spied on would be his own damned nanny.

Just as he was about to flick off the computer screen and run, Hannah said, ''You know something else, Dixon, I think your dad needs to learn how to play with you.''

Halfway out of his chair and midway to the button, he stopped and listened.

''He cooes and tickles and teases, but I think he needs to learn to really communicate with you.''

Dixon screeched.

Jake fell back into his chair and looked at the monitor. Unfortunately, the bear was still breast-high. It was like talking to a woman while forced to stare at her breasts.

''I'm sure Caro has that in a lesson plan somewhere. But I think we could move your dad into that stage more quickly if we could convince him to go to the day care with us early. If we can do that, I could pull a learning toy or two from the shelf and subtly teach him how to make the most of his time with you.''

Jake could feel his face reddening. Guilt mixed and mingled with arousal. Guilt because he was staring at her breasts as she held the bear in front of her chest. But also guilt because she was right. He had little time with his son. He needed to make the best of it.

Plus, he felt he owed her because even though his intentions were good and, up to this point, innocent, he was still spying.

He turned off the computer monitor and ran out of his office and up the steps. By the time he got to the nursery, she was stripping Dixon for his bath. Though Jake smiled at his son before he did anything else, he fought an unstoppable curiosity about Hannah's breasts. He knew a decent man would drop any and all images of them from his brain, but he had a strange desire to see if the camera had distorted them, to see what they looked like for real, to know what they felt like.

"I'll do that," Jake said, taking the advice she didn't know she had given him, by assuming Dixon's bath duties, so he could get his mind off her chest.

"That's okay, I'm fine. You can watch, though."

"No," Jake insisted, not just because he suddenly wanted to please her by doing the things she said so that she would be proud of him and realized his intentions were good if she ever discovered he had spied on her, but also because she was right. "I want to do this. I finally figured out that my time with Dixon is limited." He met her gaze, absolutely, positively determined not to look at her breasts. "I would like to make the best of it."

"Well, good for you," Hannah said, handing the baby to him.

"I also think I might take Dixon to the day care an hour early."

She gaped at him. "Really?"

"Yeah. Um… There are a couple of things I would like to talk to Caro about."

"Really? Like what? Maybe I can help you?"

Jake busied himself with removing Dixon's undershirt. "No, that's all right. We set me up in the single dad school for good reasons." *Very good reasons,* he reminded himself, fortifying his resolve before he caught Hannah's gaze. "I don't have Dixon permanently, but I will have to take care of him myself when he visits. I think it's time for me to begin to get myself accustomed to the fact that you're leaving." Even as he said the words, a horrible shaft of pain squeezed his heart, but he ignored it. Whether or not he knew what he was doing at the time, he had made the choice to live like the kind of man no woman would trust to settle down. Now he had to live with it in such a way that he didn't get his heart broken because of it.

"Yeah," she said, then licked her lips. "I guess we both should get accustomed to the fact that I'm leaving."

He nodded, scooped Dixon off the table and put him in the baby tub, focusing his attention completely on his child. His heir. A compromise gift given to him because he wasn't ever going to marry and have more kids.

"Something is definitely up with this guy," Aunt Sadie whispered in Hannah's ear. Though they were across the room from Caro and Jake, Hannah appreciated that Aunt Sadie took the precaution to make sure no one heard her comment.

Jake bounced Dixon on his lap and Hannah turned to Sadie. "Because he wants to take better care of his baby?"

"Because he keeps staring at you as if he made the biggest mistake of his life."

Hannah laughed. "I don't think so."

"I do," Sadie insisted. "Look at his body language. He's holding Dixon tightly, like he doesn't want to let him go. I'm guessing that's because he knows that when his girlfriend gets back he *has to* let him go."

Hannah conceded that with a nod. "Okay, I'll buy that. But that has nothing to do with me."

"Okay, then look at the way he's sitting in the chair. He's catty-corner. He's talking to Caro, but facing you."

Now that Sadie mentioned it, Hannah did see that.

"Interesting." She caught Sadie's gaze. "But that doesn't say anything about regretting a decision."

"No, that's in his eyes," Sadie said before she walked into the playroom and began picking up toys. "What did you two do over the weekend to make him feel so sad?"

"Nothing," Hannah said, scrambling over to her aunt so they could keep the conversation low. "He took me to Felicity's hairdresser so I could get this cut." She fingered her short, sleek cut. "Then we bought some new clothes for when I move away."

Sadie glanced down at Hannah's short shorts and new top. "Interesting that he chose casual clothes rather than work clothes."

"Oh, I bought plenty of work clothes. They're in the trunk of my car, waiting until I get a minute to take them to Mom and Dad's."

"Interesting."

Hannah sighed. "Now, how is that interesting? I simply haven't had time to drop them at Mom and Dad's yet."

"Mmm-hmm."

Hannah sighed. "Come on, Sadie. Spit it out."

"I know we already talked about what was happening between you and Jake and I know you decided against pursuing him, but it looks like Mother Nature is superseding what you decided."

If she were only remembering that Jake had almost

kissed her on Saturday night, Hannah might jump on that assessment. But because she quite painfully remembered that no matter how close they got, how many times he kissed her, how much he seemed to want her, Jake always came back to the conclusion that he couldn't get involved with her, Hannah knew it didn't matter.

"Mother Nature can supersede all she wants. Jake's not interested."

"Oh? This comes from the woman who never took her new clothes to her parents' house. You can say you didn't have time, but it seems to me that you're not taking them home because you don't intend to move home."

"I don't. At least not permanently. Once I get a job, I'll be moving to another city."

"That's worse! Leaving your new clothes in the trunk, reminding Jake that you're leaving town, and leaving him behind, is like rubbing salt into the wound."

From their conversation Sunday morning, Hannah knew it hurt Jake that she was moving. But she also knew from that very same conversation, that he wouldn't stop her. It hurt that he could like her yet still find her totally resistible. The disappointment of it made her wish she had time to sit and weep. But she didn't. There had been no promises. He had never lied. Whatever held him back, he was sticking to it.

Still, she wouldn't tell anyone any of that, and instead only stared blankly at her aunt. "Where do you come up with this stuff?"

"I've been observing the parents of children for twenty-five years and I know a sad father when I see one." She glanced at Jake again. "I've never seen him sad before. Heck, I've never seen him make a commitment like the one he's making to Dixon, or stop long enough to get advice from a pro.'' She pointed to where he sat listening to every word Caro was saying. ''I'm telling you, Hannah, you're changing him.''

Aunt Sadie paused only a second before she patted Hannah's sleek new hairdo. ''And he's changing you.''

''He's *helping* me.''

''He's *changing* you. Before Jake, you never would have even considered giving a man advice, let alone taking charge over him and his son the way you have. Whatever he's doing, he's making you more confident and that confidence is making you stronger.'' She paused, considered what she had said, then burst out laughing. ''Do you think it's possible he's making you stronger because he wants you to fight for him?''

Though she knew what her aunt was saying, Hannah deliberately misinterpreted her. ''I would never fight another woman for a man.''

''He doesn't want you to fight a woman, silly. He wants you to fight him! He wants you to fight what he's saying to you. And he's making you strong enough that you'll win.''

Though that might make a great deal of sense to her aunt, Hannah absolutely was not letting the opinion of another person interfere in this relationship. It had hurt Saturday night when he wouldn't kiss her. It hurt Sunday when he'd reinforced not wanting to get involved with her with his statement about getting accustomed to her leaving. It hurt this morning when he'd barely spoken while he'd dressed Dixon. She would have to be insane to set herself up for any more pain.

''No,'' Hannah said, and luckily one of Troy Cramer's twins squealed for help so Hannah could end the conversation.

Because in spite of how simple staying away from Jake sounded in theory, in practice, it wasn't at all easy or painless.

When they returned that afternoon, Jake handed Dixon to Hannah with the instruction to put him down for his nap, then he raced to his office and the NannyCam. He listened to her tell Dixon she approved of everything he had done that day at the day care, and a huge smile lit his face. He didn't care to investigate further why pleasing her meant to so much to him. He knew why. He also knew those feelings were going to make the pain of losing her more intense. But he just kept telling himself he was doing this for Dixon.

In fact, he turned it into something of a mantra the next morning and the morning after that and the morning after that as he sat in his office with his first cup of coffee every day to listen to her talk to Dixon. Each day he observed her for ten minutes as she talked to his little boy, listening to her praise what he had done the day before and her suggestions for what he should do that day. Then he would leave his desk, run up the steps and enter the nursery as if he had just finished his shower.

Every day he bathed Dixon, dressed the baby, took him to the kitchen, found the bib and fed him.

And every day Hannah's grin of approval grew.

"He adores you!" she said on Sunday morning, her smile wistful and beautiful.

"Well, I love him, too." Jake paused, the spoon about midway to Dixon's mouth. "I finally saw that I had to make the best of every minute whenever he was here.''

''That's great. You've come so far.''

Jake almost said, ''So have you,'' but he stopped himself. Because he recognized all he was really saying was that she was now ready to leave him. She had become a confident woman. Someone who could hold her own anywhere she went. Someone who didn't need him anymore.

''Oh, I almost forgot to tell you. I sent out résumés to all the Pittsburgh area schools yesterday.''

A knife twisted in his gut. ''Oh. Are they looking for teachers?''

She grimaced. ''No. But I'm hoping that in one of the school districts a teacher might unexpectedly quit, retire or find work elsewhere.''

''Right,'' he said because he knew one would. In a city the size of Pittsburgh someone was always leaving and she would probably have no trouble finding a job. That realization twisted the knife in his gut again. It was the beginning of the end. First she would find a job. Then she would go apartment hunting in her little denim miniskirts and halter tops. Then she would make friends. Scope out her new neighborhood. Find the pub. Accidentally stumble on the local softball team's watering hole. Be hit on by every jock there. Probably go on dates.

Maybe find just the right guy.

Date him exclusively.

Get engaged.

Marry him.

The knife twisted again.

Just as she had changed Jake into the perfect father

for Dixon, he had helped her to change her into the perfect woman for some lucky man.

And the realization finally hit him full-force that though it wasn't going to be him, it was going to be *somebody*.

Somebody else was going to marry this woman who was so perfect for him.

Chapter Eight

At Caro and Max's wedding reception the next week, Hannah stood at the shiny oak bar staring at Jake. In the dim light of the banquet room, she watched him as he worked the crowd as one of Max's groomsmen. In spite of the July heat, he was comfortable in his tuxedo, holding Dixon, greeting some guests, stopping to chat with others. He was so gosh-darned good-looking, so confident, and so interesting, that it was hard not to simply enjoy watching him.

"Come on, Hannah, the photographer wants the bride and her sisters by the cake for one more picture."

Hannah smiled at her sister Sadie, who looked stunning in the coral-and-yellow floral gown Caro had chosen for all of her bridesmaids. Though they all wore the same dress, against Sadie's tanned skin the gown was sexy. On Maria, whose long hair seemed to tangle with the flowers, it was exotic. But on Hannah the dress was regal. With her hair swept away from her face by a rhinestone comb, and a single gold chain accenting her slender neck, she was the picture of elegance. And she knew it.

For the first time in her life she knew she was beautiful. Graceful. She looked more sophisticated than she really was, but, in the flowing gown Hannah found it completely possible to act as worldly as the gown made her appear.

Jake had taught her a lot. But it was knowing she had to leave town, knowing it really was time for her to stand on her own two feet, that had pushed her into redefining her world, her preconceived notions about life, and even her definition of herself. She was different because she was taking responsibility for herself. She was more confident, and it showed.

"Hannah!" Sadie called impatiently.

"Okay, I'm sorry! I'm coming," she said, following Sadie across the crowded floor of the unexpectedly ornate banquet room of the country club. Green Hills, once a hunting retreat, had been purchased by a corporation that had turned the surrounding forest into a golf course and the lodge into a clubhouse. The lodge had been remodeled into a locker room and bar for the golfers, and a wing had been added to create the restaurant and banquet hall.

Sadie and Hannah slid under the lily-covered trellis that took them to the cake table, as Caro and Max posed for pictures beside it. Caro was perfect in her strapless, white beaded gown. And Max was elegant and masterful in his black tie and tails. Still, Hannah thought as she walked toward her sister and brand new brother-in-law, nobody in the room compared to Jake. The man was born to be at ease with wealth and power.

"Why don't you ask Troy's friend Skip Wellington to dance?" Sadie whispered in her ear as she, Maria, Caro and Hannah formed a semicircle behind the tall white-rosebud cake. "Rumor has it, he's going to be handling the presidential campaign for Art Carrington next spring. If you play your cards right, you could be married to the White House Chief of Staff."

"No way!" Caro gasped, two seconds after the photographer took his shot. She grabbed Hannah's hand and tugged her away from Sadie. "I think she should ask Cory Donnelly. He's younger. He's better looking. And he's not in politics."

"Politics isn't a dirty word," Sadie said with a laugh.

But Hannah noticed Jake scanning the crowd. His gaze unerringly found hers and he smiled.

"Besides, since Hannah is now an absolute beauty queen with her cute new hairdo and great makeup thanks to the mystery beautician Jake won't tell us about, I think she should set her sights a little higher."

"A little higher than a future chief of staff?" Sadie asked incredulously.

Hannah saw Jake hand Dixon to his mother, who eagerly took him.

Caro laughed. "You think marrying a politician is setting one's sights high?"

"It is when the guy will someday be the guy who helps the leader of the free world!"

Jake began to walk toward her. Hannah's lips lifted into a smile.

"But Cory is more her own age."

"That's exactly what makes him too young for her. She needs someone a few years older. Someone settled. Skippy is settled."

At last Jake reached her. He held out his hand. "Dance?"

"Yes!" Hannah said, rolling her eyes in the direction of her arguing sisters. "Save me."

Jake chuckled and tugged lightly on her fingers to get her to the dance floor. When she was in his arms he said, "You look amazing."

Feeling happy and confident, like an adult who could accept Jake's decision not to get involved with her, Hannah decided to have fun and to enjoy the time she had with him. She tilted her head back to catch his gaze. "Oh, you like this old thing?"

Jake's gaze dipped between them to rest pointedly on the V of her dress that exposed a long strip of cleavage.

"Yeah, I really like that 'old thing.'"

Hannah laughed. "You just like that it reveals too darned much cleavage."

He caught her gaze and to Hannah it seemed as if he debated his answer, but eventually he cautiously said, "No. It kind of makes me feel warm and romantic."

Hannah lifted a brow. "Really?"

"Yeah."

Two weeks ago she would have thought that a declaration of love. Tonight she saw his statement for what it was. Reality. They liked each other. They had no future, but they enjoyed each other's company. Was it so bad to give in to that, if only for a little while?

"I never took you for the warm, romantic type. I always thought you were more the black-satin-and-lace kind." She tilted her head and studied him. "The wild, adventurous kind."

"I am."

He spun her around once, and the quick movement reminded Jake of the dance they had shared at his birthday. He remembered thinking she was fresh and funny, but shy. Tonight, she was fresh and funny, but also warm and familiar. And he simply wasn't in the mood to fight it anymore.

He caught her gaze. "But romance can be exciting, too."

She considered that. "In its way."

"And it doesn't have to lead to anything permanent."

Her smile faltered a little so Jake hurried on. "It also doesn't have to lead to sex."

That made her laugh. "Too bad."

He almost stopped dancing. "I mean it, Hannah. Your brother would skin me alive if he thought I took advantage of you."

"Who says you would be taking advantage of me?"

She said it as "mature" Hannah, the woman he was seeing more and more of lately, and everything in his body seemed to spring to attention. But he knew that no matter what she said, taking the night to that final "big" conclusion was wrong.

"Let's just put it this way. That's got to be off limits for us. But I like you. I really like you. And for one night I would like to have you all to myself."

His words shot electricity down Hannah's spine, but remembering that tonight she was regal and elegant, not naive and fanciful, she glanced around as if bored, then brought her gaze back to his and smiled. "Kind of hard for you to have me all to yourself when we're in a room full of people."

"That's what makes it so safe. Knowing your

brother is right over there,'' he said, nodding toward the bar and her tall, broad, fair-haired brother. ''Knowing he'd slap me silly and send you to a convent if he thought we were getting too chummy will keep us within the bounds of propriety.'' He paused, searched her eyes. ''Be with me tonight, Hannah. Have fun with me.''

It was very hard to resist a man who wanted nothing more than the pleasure of her company and very hard to ignore the warmth that curled through her middle when he spoke to her that way. Particularly since she had already made this decision even before he'd made the proposal. But Hannah took a few seconds to study the look in his eyes before replying. Not to pretend she was more sophisticated than she was, but because there was something there. Not something dark and sinister. Not even something sexual. But *something*.

''How good of a dancer are you?''

''I'm an exceptional dancer.'' He twirled her once to remind her of that.

''Then I'm yours for the night.'' She paused, glanced around, then asked, ''What about Dixon?''

''My mother is taking him back to my house at around nine. She promised to have him in bed before I get home.''

''Okay, that about settles it.'' She smiled at him, not sure she should ignore the secret ''something'' in the depths of his eyes, but somehow knowing that the willingness to do so—not so much for herself, but for him—was what separated the girls from the women. And tonight she was a woman.

That might have settled everything for Hannah, but it did nothing to settle the nerves in Jake's stomach.

He told himself he wasn't leading her on and from her easy acceptance of the idea that they spend this evening together, Jake knew he wasn't. The problem was, he was leading himself on. Not only was she going to leave Wilburn and leave him to move on to bigger and better things, but he was also tempting himself with something he couldn't have.

Still, he didn't stop himself from directing her out to the patio when the band took a break. But when they got there, they weren't alone. The warm night inspired most of the wedding guests to stroll out the double glass doors of the country club banquet room. Jake took Hannah's hand and guided her along a lit stone path.

"Where are we going?" she asked, laughing as he all but dragged her down a slight incline. Her light floral dress lifted in the July breeze. The scent of the forest filled the air.

"Just trust me."

"In two-hundred-dollar shoes and a dress that shouldn't touch dirt? I'm having trouble with that."

Jake laughed, tugged her three or four more feet, just beyond the glow of the last light on the path, and into a garden. Realizing they were in complete darkness, he stopped abruptly and turned around, but his movement was so quick Hannah didn't have a chance to anticipate it and plowed right into his chest.

"Whoa!" he said, steadying her with his hands on her shoulders.

"Whoa yourself! You should come with brake lights."

Jake laughed until he suddenly realized how close they were. Though they had been dancing together all night, they had been in the semi-lit company of three hundred other celebrating people. Now, here they were in the dark, with his hands on her naked shoulders, close enough that all he would have to do is lower his head and he could kiss her.

Even in the dark, he could see her green eyes shining up at him. He noticed emotion flicker through them and he guessed she realized the same thing he had. They were alone, in the dark, almost pressed together.

Still, she didn't move. She didn't run. She didn't suggest they get back to the crowd. She only stared at him, her eyes darkened with appreciation, her lips trembling in a slight smile.

Feelings and sensations washed through Jake. He had never felt this way about anyone before. Protective. Exasperated. Attracted. Lured. And curious. Oh, she made him curious about so many things. About being a dad, about settling down, about what kinds of thoughts danced around in that pretty head of hers.

She blinked and he found himself being drawn forward. The first time they had kissed, it was an accident. The second time they had kissed, it was more of an experiment. Now, he wanted to kiss Hannah Evans just because he wanted to kiss her.

His head continued its descent. She didn't flinch or move or stop him. Instead, in the last second before their mouths met, her eyelids drifted shut. Jake touched his mouth to hers.

And a million sensations shot through him. First and foremost he was overwhelmed with the knowledge that this was Hannah. Sweet, beautiful, incredibly wonderful Hannah.

She tasted like champagne and lipstick, and again, desire and need ricocheted through him. Jake used every ounce of his self-control to keep from deepening the kiss, but she shifted to get closer, her dress rustling in the quiet night, and his arm involuntarily tightened around her waist, bringing her closer still.

He felt the press of her breasts as they flattened against his shirt and another frisson of excitement skittered through him. Losing another notch of control, he cupped the back of her head and deepened their kiss, his tongue tumbling into her mouth, finding hers to mate with it.

Crickets chirped around them. A bullfrog croaked. The scent of the nearby pond wafted to them, somehow romanticizing the kiss even more. As their mouths mated, their tongues twining wetly, their bodies seeking to get ever closer, Jake felt himself being drawn further and further into the abyss of need. He slid his hands down her naked back and wished for a million things he knew he couldn't have. As he savored her sweetness and all but devoured Hannah's mouth, Jake had to face reality. He was a runaround. A womanizer. It wasn't a matter of whether or not she wanted him. The truth was, she *deserved* better.

That really was the bottom line. He did not deserve her. And she deserved everything.

Slowly, with regret, he backed away.

She blinked up at him, her eyes passion glazed.

"We better go back."

The words came out on a hoarse whisper that drifted across the dew of the darkened garden, and the light of understanding lit her sleepy eyes. She swallowed hard. "Yeah."

He took her hand and led her back up the path. Music floated down to them, indicating that the band had begun to play again. A quick glance at the patio showed that most of the wedding guests had returned inside to dance.

He guided her to the doors, then dropped her hand and smiled at her to break the mood before they entered her sister's wedding reception and encountered the hundreds of eyes that would be checking them out. "How are those two-hundred-dollar shoes doing?"

When disappointment flickered through her soft green eyes, a band of regret tightened his chest. He knew she wanted what they shared in the garden to be forever. He knew she didn't understand why it couldn't. He wanted to say "I'm sorry," but couldn't bring himself to say it because he wasn't sure he was sorry. He wasn't sure "sorry" was the appropriate way to describe how he felt. He was who he was. He couldn't change his past or what he had been or even what he wanted out of his life. So he couldn't be *sorry*.

He turned and guided her into the wedding festivities again. Something told him to take her to the bar where her sister Sadie and brother-in-law Troy stood laughing with a crowd. Something else told him to take her to the table where Luke sat with her parents, Pete and Lily. To leave her with either one of her siblings where she would be safe. Instead, he turned onto the dance floor, pulled her into his arms and tightly against him. When she didn't argue or protest, he rested his chin on top of her head and felt an agony of emotions. He savored the closeness, the fact that their evening wasn't over, the fact that she still wanted him even as he despaired that he could not have her.

She slipped away a few minutes before Caro threw her bouquet and Jake watched her deliberately avoid catching it. He couldn't stop a smile, thinking she wouldn't want marriage by superstition. He watched her wave goodbye when Caro and Max ran out the door on their way to a honeymoon and a new life. All the time he studied the wistful look in her eyes. Part of him was infuriated that choices he had made at eighteen and lived out for the past fifteen years didn't fit or work for a man of thirty-three who wanted this woman more and more with each passing day.

The other part was infuriated with himself for pining over something he couldn't have because he knew, had always known, these choices were right. He was who he was. A man very much like his father. A man who couldn't settle down.

A wife like Felicity might have been able to accept a few years of marital bliss that ended in an amicable divorce when he got bored, as his father had gotten bored. But a wife like Hannah would never accept it. She would never understand it. It would always haunt her. He also knew that if he could get himself away from temptation and stop questioning himself, he would be fine.

So he turned from Hannah and temptation and left the reception, ending the internal arguments, saving himself and Hannah from making any more mistakes.

When he arrived home, he found his mother and Larry in his living room watching the end of a movie. He chatted with them for a few minutes about the lovely wedding, then thanked them for caring for Dixon before they left.

Then Jake was all alone in his big, big house. He had everything a man could want, including a son, his heir—technically, his own family—yet he was lonely. For the first time in his life he felt wrong.

Absolutely wrong. As though every choice he had ever made had been wrong. As though every thought

SUSAN MEIER 137

he had ever had was wrong. Because they had led him to this minute of severe emptiness.

He told himself that that couldn't be true. Because if it was true for him, then it would have been true for his father, too. If every choice Jake made was wrong, then every choice his father had made was wrong, and Jake wouldn't be able to forgive his father for leaving him and his mother...and not loving them enough.

His front door creaked open and Jake jumped. Not the kind of person to cower in the dark, afraid of the unknown, he bounced from his sofa and ran to the foyer only to find Hannah.

Clearly startled, she peeked up at him, with two fingers on the back strap of one of her shoes, frozen in the middle of taking it off. "Hi."

His heart clenched. "Hi." He took two steps toward her then forced himself to stop. "I thought you would be staying at your parents' house tonight?"

She laughed. "And who would get up with Dixon?"

Jake had the good graces to smile sheepishly. "I was hoping he would sleep through the night."

"No. He won't. That's why you hired me and that's why I'm here."

"Yeah, you are." He studied her pretty, tousled blond hair, her big green eyes, the plump pink lips he had kissed only a few hours before, and wished with all his heart he could be the man she needed, the man she deserved. Not just because she was sweet and beautiful and wonderful, but because she was good, kind and responsible. She deserved somebody who could give her as much as she gave to everybody else.

He ran his hand along her jawline, so tempted to kiss her his lips tingled with need. But he couldn't.

He *wouldn't*. He didn't want to lead her on. He didn't want to be led on himself. She was leaving. They both knew it. Hoping she didn't find a man in Pittsburgh was wrong…and selfish.

He stepped away. "Good night, Hannah."

She turned toward the stairway, her floral gown swishing and flowing around her. "Good night."

Hannah climbed the steps as quickly as possible and all but ran down the hall. She jumped into her room, closed the door behind her, leaned against it and squeezed her eyes shut.

Damn the man.

Did he have to be so gorgeous?

Did he have to be so sweet?

Did he have to be so desperately open about how much he needed to be loved?

That was the something she had seen in his eyes. He needed to be loved. If his behavior and reactions were anything to go by Hannah would even guess that for some reason or another he felt he didn't deserve to be loved. But that wasn't true! It couldn't be true. He was wonderful, and when he faltered, when he chose not to kiss her, he made her long to prove he did deserve to be loved. He brought out every protective, loving instinct she had, even as he made her weak with desire.

And if she didn't get away from him soon, she would be so madly in love with him and he would hurt her. Not because he didn't want to love her but because he couldn't.

Because he didn't feel he deserved to be loved, he had convinced himself he was in love with his job, in love with his life, and Hannah knew he really believed that. She wasn't foolish enough to think that he could be magically transformed by someone like her.

A simple girl.

A small-town girl.

Who, really, if push came to shove, was only figuring out how to help herself. She didn't have the experience, the knowledge or the power to help him. All she could do was watch his sadness when she walked away.

Chapter Nine

The next morning Jake found himself drawn to the NannyCam. Quietly, without fanfare, he flicked on his computer screen and immediately the full nursery came into view. From its perch on the eye-level shelf, the bear transmitted everything Hannah did as she prepared Dixon for the day.

Lowering himself to the tall-backed office chair behind him, Jake watched her hum softly to his baby boy, watched her smile at Dixon, saw the unmitigated glow caring for his son gave her, and cursed softly. Even though he had rejected her the night before, she wasn't letting the loss get in the way of caring for his son. She was intelligent. She was beautiful. She was wonderful. And he couldn't have her.

"I wonder where your daddy is," she said to Dixon as she pulled him from his baby tub and wrapped him in a blanket towel. "I thought he had gotten accustomed to being with you first thing in the morning.

It's the best part of the day and the best way to start a day, by seeing the people you love.''

Jake swallowed. Technically, he was seeing the people he loved, the people he wanted in his life more than anybody else. And that was the problem. He wasn't supposed to have feelings for Hannah. But he did and it was his own fault. Thinking he had everything under control, he'd spent time with her while she cared for his son, which had paved the way for other deeper, stronger feelings.

But he hadn't realized that until those feelings surfaced at the wedding. Though he resisted them, they'd haunted him with dreams that had awakened him aroused and needy. He'd tossed and turned all night with desire. Not just for sex—though he wanted that—but for all those other things she'd made him feel. Things he knew he couldn't have.

He understood the only way to fix this mess would be to stay away from her completely. Unfortunately, that meant he couldn't be with her in the morning with Dixon, couldn't watch her as she cared for his son, couldn't learn the things she had been teaching him. But even as he had that thought, Jake knew that wasn't true because he was staring at her right now—through the NannyCam. He had been doing this for weeks and he could continue to do it. He simply couldn't go to the nursery to try out her advice when she was there.

Deciding he was an absolute genius, Jake jotted down her comment about seeing Dixon first thing in the morning, the way he would make notes at any business meeting—one eye on the meeting's participants, one eye on his notepad. Because he couldn't put her suggestions into practice while they were fresh in his mind, he knew notes were his only option.

"I think if your dad were smart, he would become your Little League coach."

He jotted that down.

"That way he has more of a motivation to drop his work for a few hours and be with you."

True enough, Jake thought, scribbling the word motivation. He knew how he was. Hell, he knew how *every* workaholic was. When they got involved in something, it was hard to put it down, no matter what the clock said. Understanding this side of himself had eventually helped him to understand his father, but it was one part of his dad's personality Jake knew he would never fall victim to. He would never allow Dixon to feel there was something wrong with him since his own father couldn't attend his ball games.

That made him frown until he saw that Hannah was snuggling Dixon close and his son was crying. Jake had no idea what had made the little boy cry, but he experienced a jolt to the stomach seeing it.

"Oh, don't cry, honey," Hannah crooned. "You'll be okay."

"What happened?" Jake asked the question as he leaned forward.

"It's a just a little bump."

"From what!"

"And lots of babies smack themselves in the eye. You just don't have all the muscle control you need yet."

Relieved, Jake sat back in his seat. But as his relief abated another set of emotions enveloped him. He loved seeing Hannah with Dixon. He loved seeing her snuggle him, comfort him, kiss him. He swallowed hard. Learning via the NannyCam might physically distance him from Hannah, but it wasn't really keeping him away from her. If anything, he was seeing an even more intimate view of her because she was in her natural state, perfectly comfortable and relaxed with Dixon.

He rose from his tall-backed black leather office chair, and crumpled up the piece of paper on which he had been taking notes, knowing that he couldn't do this, and also knowing he could remember everything she said.

Because he would remember everything she had ever said to him. And he knew for his sake as well as for hers he had to do something to get her out of his mind, out of his thoughts, out of his blood.

He had to put a stop to this infatuation of theirs once and for all.

On Monday morning, when Hannah entered the day care, she noticed everything seemed to stop. Not the kids, of course. They were in perpetual motion. Scattered around the big, open room, they laughed, talked and fought over toys. The adults were the ones who seemed to come to a quick halt. Looks passed between her aunt and her sisters. Unspoken thoughts were communicated with sidelong glances.

"So, what happened?" Sadie asked the second she reached Hannah at the door. Marie was on her heels. Her big brown eyes round with curiosity. If Caro hadn't been on her honeymoon, Hannah knew she would be right behind them.

"What happened about what?" Hannah asked, setting Dixon's travel seat on the countertop so she could lift him out and snuggle him against her cheek.

"With you and Jake?"

Her and Jake. Hearing them paired together like

that seemed so natural, so right. Yet on Saturday night he had confirmed that he might like her—heck, from the pained look in his eyes when he'd told her goodnight, Hannah would almost guess he absolutely loved her—but he wouldn't get into a relationship with her. Then on Sunday, he'd deserted her. He'd instructed her to take the day off, then scooped up Dixon and headed for parts unknown. When she returned after eight, Dixon was already in bed and Jake was sequestered in the master suite. He hadn't even left a note to say good-night. Worse, this morning he had left the house before she'd awakened. From the way the blankets were neatly tucked around Dixon, she could tell that Jake had made a quick morning visit, which proved it was Hannah he was avoiding.

Because that hurt and confused her, Hannah had an urge to confide in her older sisters. She loved them and she knew they loved her and would comfort her. But more than that, they could probably give her very good advice.

But just at the point when she would have opened her mouth to speak, another thought struck her. Everything that had happened between her and Jake on Saturday night was heartbreakingly intimate. There was no way she could describe to her sisters the intensity of her love for Jake, or the intensity of her longing to be part of his life. There was no way she could explain how she knew that it hurt him not to be able to love her. And there was no way she could explain that she also knew beyond a shadow of a doubt that there was a very good, very strong reason he couldn't love her.

Why? Because he had never told her that reason, or even that there was a reason, beyond not wanting to get involved with his best friend's little sister. It was merely an instinct she had. But the bond between her and Jake was so intense that they didn't always have to speak to communicate. He knew it from the first "please" she had transmitted with her eyes to get him to hire her. She knew it every time he did the right thing with Dixon. She barely had to explain anything to him anymore. He always seemed to realize what his next step should be.

And she didn't want to tell her sisters that, either.

Not because she was afraid they would laugh at her, correct her, or give her bad advice, but because the thing between her and Jake was so private she didn't want to violate it.

"I'm Jake's nanny," she said, when she normally would have fallen onto a chair by the desk and spilled all her secrets. But some kind of invisible line had been drawn and she couldn't cross it. "And he is my boss. In the course of things, we've become friends."

She caught her sister Sadie's gaze, then Maria's. "Really good friends. If you saw anything between us Saturday night, it was friendship. And that's all there is to tell."

Sadie gave her a confused look. Marie cocked her head in question. Aunt Sadie ambled over from the toy box.

"Hannah, I'm going to need some special help from you today, if you don't mind."

Hannah spun to face her. "Sure, Aunt Sadie. Anything you want."

"Good, Maria's teaching Caro's single dad class this morning, so Sadie and the twins can take care of Dixon."

"Okay," Hannah replied, handing Dixon to Sadie,

who held out her arms to take the little boy. "What do you need?"

Sadie turned Hannah toward the makeshift office in the corner. Her computer was on, the cursor blinking. "Well, I'm developing some structured playtime for the kids with ages between eight and ten for the after-school hours this fall."

Hannah laughed. "It's July."

"It never hurts to be prepared. Since you're an elementary teacher, I figured you could help me."

"I'm happy to."

"Good," Aunt Sadie said, though Hannah noticed she was watching Maria and Sadie as they went back to their work with the kids. When everyone seemed to be settled, Aunt Sadie quickly turned to Hannah.

"I'm not going to ask you for details," Aunt Sadie said, taking Hannah's hand. "But I saw something really special happening with you and Jake at the wedding. And this morning, when your sisters pounced but you deflected their questions, I saw something else. Intimacy. Only a woman who has been intimate with a man will keep his secrets."

Hannah squeezed her aunt's fingers. "First, he hasn't told me his secrets. Second, I haven't slept with him."

"You don't have to sleep with a man to be intimate. And, Hannah, that's really what's happening here. You're forming a bond of trust so strong, it's superseding your relationship with your sisters."

Hannah swallowed. "Are you telling me that's good?"

"It's good in terms of the fact that it's a sign that you're growing up, but bad because you're growing away."

"Growing away isn't always bad, Aunt Sadie."
Hannah caught her aunt's gaze. "I have to grow away
from them. I can't constantly depend on my sisters for
advice and help. I have to learn to stand on my own
two feet because pretty soon I'm going to be moving
to Pittsburgh."

Aunt Sadie shook her head. "You're just going to
leave him like this?"

Hannah busied herself with some papers on Sadie's
desk. "Like what?"

"Alone. Hurt. Sad. You know as well as I do that
he's sad."

Hannah sighed. "Yes, I do."

"And you're not going to try to find out why?"

"Aunt Sadie, he doesn't tell me anything. He walks
away, or steps away, or emotionally distances himself
every time we get close." She caught her aunt's gaze.
"I have feelings too. The guy has told me more than
once he doesn't want me. I'm not sure I can take it
again."

"I can understand that," Sadie said sympatheti-
cally. "But there are two sides to every decision and
the other side to this one is, can you live with yourself
knowing that you somehow opened a can of worms
for him that he can't seem to handle?"

No, Hannah thought, driving home that afternoon,
I'm not sure I can. However, she wasn't exactly sure
she knew how to have a deep, dark discussion about
a man's heartrending feelings, either. She had never
done this before and, without her sisters's help, she
didn't know if she could set the mood or bring her
and Jake to the kind of situation that would make him
comfortable enough to talk to her.

But when Dixon grabbed one of his bottles from the diaper bag, which she had hastily packed because she was so preoccupied, and tossed it to the front seat of her car, spraying formula all over her dashboard, Hannah was suddenly inspired. There was no way she would yell at an innocent child for that. And there was no way Jake would get angry or dismiss her if she played on his sympathies. Better yet, if she played on his sympathies before she tried to get him to talk, he might just spill his guts without her having to pry anything out of him.

Her plan formed quickly. She made lasagna because her lasagna was stringy and watery, and could actually be more accurately described as awful. There was no way Jake would yell at her, dismiss her, or ignore her after she proudly served him a terrible dinner. He wouldn't have the heart. She didn't exactly want him to feel sorry for her, but she did want to disarm him. Her stringy lasagna could bring anyone to their knees.

Then she arranged Dixon's eating schedule so that he would be done and in bed by eight, which was when she intended to serve dinner. By now she knew that Jake would come home late because he would be trying to avoid her, so she would be ready for him by being a minute or two later.

Just as she'd predicted, Jake didn't return home until a little after eight. He apologized. She smiled.

"That's okay. I suspected you would be late so dinner's just getting done now."

His mouth dropped slightly.

Disarming process in progress. Neutral expression crumbling.

"You made dinner?"

"Sure. Just like I have been. You have half an hour

to get a shower and change if you like, then I thought we could eat on the patio.''

He licked his lips, clearly tense and stalling. Hannah could tell he knew he should be getting out of this, but he didn't have a clue how. She almost laughed. Wait until he saw the cheese stretch from the spatula to his plate like a high wire over a circus ring. He would be helpless!

Again, Hannah desperately wanted to laugh. But she didn't. Tonight she was a woman going after what she wanted. He had something important to tell her. She wasn't letting him get away until he did. The process to disarm him was moving along nicely. She would be maturely patient.

He took a long breath and Hannah knew an excuse was coming. But no matter what he said, no matter what excuse he gave to avoid her, she had an answer for him.

''I have a date.''

That wasn't on her list of possible avoidance tactics! She just barely held back a gasp of shock. ''What?''

Jake combed his fingers through his hair. ''I'm sorry, Hannah,'' he said, and met her gaze across the space of the foyer. ''Really.'' Every nerve ending in his body had sprung to life, partially because of the way she was dressed. In her little white top and cute capri pants, with her hair bouncing around her face, she looked adorable. But her take-charge attitude was that of a woman, and that was what he found irresistible. That was why his nerve endings hummed. That was also why he had a date. He didn't merely need to get away from her, he wanted her to see him for what he was, a man who dated lots of women.

''You have a date?'' she asked incredulously.

"It was a spur of the moment thing. A friend of Troy's in from California."

"Oh."

"I'm sorry," he said again, and wished he hadn't. Not because he wasn't sorry, but because he liked this mature, vibrant woman who knew what she wanted and this "sorry" had nothing to do with regret for hurting her and everything to do with regret for what he was missing.

And that took him back into the dangerous territory he wasn't allowed to travel into. He could not date, like or romance this woman because to him she spelled commitment, permanency, family, roots. All the things he couldn't have.

He edged past her to go to the stairs. "I'm sorry about dinner," he said as neutrally as he could. "Maybe we can freeze it."

With that he walked up the steps and didn't let himself stop or think the entire time he showered and dressed for his date with Troy's personal accountant's secretary. The woman was twenty-nine and sweet like Hannah, but in a more polished way. She wasn't looking for a husband, no mistake on that score, and he desperately needed a diversion.

But when he picked up Julianna Johnson, Jake also started picking up all kinds of odd signals. She didn't want to go out for dinner. He had to say he was starving and hated hotel food, just to get her out the door. Then all she wanted was to go back to the hotel. She wasn't interested in the sights or local culture. Nope. She just wanted to go back to her hotel room. And from the way she wrapped herself around his neck, Jake knew exactly why.

By the time he dropped her off around midnight—

having just barely talked himself out of being forced to enter her hotel room with her—he wondered what in the hell both Troy and Hannah's sister Sadie thought of him to hook him up with this jaded, not-even-slightly-subtle woman.

He entered his foyer tired, concluding that Troy and Sadie thought he was a cynical old man. Not only had Julianna all but told him she'd only wanted him for sex, but Troy and Sadie apparently didn't think Jake would balk at her behavior.

Heading for his office and a few minutes to think, Jake recognized that the unfortunate truth was that he had given everybody the impression women like Julianna were the types of women he liked. But turning on his monitor and watching the NannyCam pictures come into view, seeing Hannah in Dixon's room, tucking him in after feeding him a bottle, Jake knew everything had changed. Except the important thing. He still couldn't have it. What he wanted was very, very different, but now he suffered the torment of the damned because he still couldn't have it.

As he removed his suit jacket and slid off his tie, he watched Hannah kiss Dixon's forehead. Jake smiled softly. She backed away from the crib and headed for the door. Jake sighed, rose from his seat and headed for his office sofa. He had to think through how he would survive the next few weeks.

Hoping to figure out how to stop wanting Hannah, he lay down on his sofa and closed his eyes, forcing himself to consider what a relationship with Hannah would really be like. It certainly wouldn't be hit or miss and flippant, like the affairs he had had with other women. She would want all of his attention. She would want to know all his secrets. She would demand

all of his passion. But she would also give him all of
hers. They would be equal. They would be passionate.
It would be the most intimate, intense relationship a
man could handle. Even though that scared Jake, it
also shot a challenge through his blood, a sexual/emo-
tional challenge so tempting his mouth began to water
with the unexpected enticement of it. His blood sang
in his veins. His heart pounded.

"Hey."

Jake bounced up on his sofa at the sound of Hannah's voice at his doorway.

She strolled into his office. "What are you doing?"

Heart-pounding challenge still singing through his
veins, Jake swallowed and tried to look normal. "Just
thinking. What are you doing?"

"Dixon got up. I put him back to sleep."

Jake almost said, "I know," but he stopped himself
just in time. The reason he knew was that he had
watched her on his NannyCam. And the monitor was
still on! She couldn't see it, positioned as it was on
the side rest of his desk. But if she stepped one foot
to the right, the screen would be in her line of vision
and she would know he had been watching her. Dear
God! The last thing she needed to discover right now
was that he had been spying on her! She was already
going to hate him when she found a job in Pittsburgh
and he let her slide out of his life. There was no point
in having her absolutely despise him.

He captured her complete attention with his world-
famous disarming smile. He had to. He was desperate.
"Why aren't *you* going back to sleep?"

She shrugged. "I was a little worried about you."

He laughed lightly. "There's nothing to worry
about."

She sat beside him on the sofa and though Jake was relieved that she could no longer see his computer screen, his breath caught just from being this close to her. The lure of the dare of a relationship with her sprang up inside him again, reminding him that a good challenge was the one thing in life he couldn't resist.

She bestowed her sweet smile upon him. "I think there is."

Jake swallowed hard and all his nerve endings went on red alert. She was beautiful, sleep-tousled and within reach. And she knew him. Her soft words held no speculation, no nuance of probing. She straightfor-wardly said what she had to say, reminding him that theirs would be a completely honest, completely open relationship. The challenge of it spiked in his blood again. He knew he couldn't be what she wanted him to be. But the uncertainty of the dare was what made it so enticing.

"I'm fine."

"What if I told you *I* wasn't fine?"

The question took Jake so much by surprise that he faced her. If anybody so much as looked cross-eyed at her, Jake would rip him limb from limb. If someone actually did something to hurt her, Jake wasn't sure he could be responsible for what he would do. "What's wrong?"

She took a quick breath, then her tongue darted out to moisten her lips. Jake's insides began to quiver and he realized again how precariously close they were. With one swipe of his hand he could catch the back of her neck, yank her to him and kiss her senseless.

"I like you and I know you like me and I don't understand why you're backing away."

He swallowed. Right now backing away was the

very last thing on his mind. Which was exactly why he couldn't speak. He wasn't sure he would have control over what he said, or if words of love and need would spill from him.

"I know you told me you were afraid of Luke in the beginning. But that's over now. We're beyond that." She caught his gaze with her beautiful green eyes and Jake's heart pounded in his chest. "We like each other a lot. When you kiss me, I melt in your arms. Sexually, we would probably set your house on fire." She laid her hand on his forearm, setting little wildfires of excitement on his skin. "Yet, you don't want me."

She held his gaze and Jake saw the horrible disappointment there, the pain of rejection, the shadow of self-doubt, and every male instinct to protect her surged to life. They mixed and mingled with his sexual desire for her, causing him to feel he should show her how much he wanted her, erase her doubts and ease his need.

"Why don't you want me?"

Jake took a long shuddering breath and prayed for strength. "I *do* want you. That's the problem. I'm not supposed to want you and you're not supposed to want me. I went out with Julianna tonight to get you—to get *us*—to stop thinking of each other in romantic terms."

"Why? We're both adults."

"Yeah, but I'm so much older than you are, Hannah. Not just in age, but also in experience. I've know things… I've *done* things you wouldn't even yet think to dream about."

She laughed merrily. "Lucky me."

That made him groan. "Don't say that!"

"Why? America is full of double standards and this is one of them. Women want their men experienced."

She slid closer on the sofa. Jake could almost feel heat emanating from her. His heartbeat jumped to triple time. The muscles in his stomach tightened and expanded.

She brushed her fingers across his cheek. "I could really, really love you. And I sense you feel the same about me. So why don't we just dive into this and see what happens?"

As she said the last she placed her hand on the back of Jake's head and tipped him forward, bringing him close enough that she could kiss him.

And everything inside Jake snapped. She was soft and warm. Her mouth was incredibly willing and he was hungry. For weeks he had been denying himself—denying *this*—and he was done denying. He had an intense attraction to this woman that was part physical and part emotional, and he couldn't resist the combination.

He curved his hand around her neck and brought her closer to devour her mouth. As delightfully wicked desires danced in his brain, he reminded himself that not only was Hannah Luke's little sister, she was also an inexperienced woman with whom he would have to go slow.

But just as quickly as he had that thought, another one canceled it out. *This* was what he wanted from her. The passion. The pleasure. All wrapped up and kept proper by intense emotions. He wasn't yet ready to call any of those emotions love, but they were deep, strong. If she couldn't handle this, if she couldn't love him and want him the way he needed her to want and love him, then pushing her to see that was a quick, easy way out for both of them. Then, he wouldn't have to admit anything about his father. Then, he wouldn't have to admit he didn't believe he could be faithful. He wouldn't have to admit he would probably end up hurting her.

This was the perfect way out for both of them. While he was hungry and she thought she was willing, they would test whether she really was as ready as she thought. They would be able to end this before he had to confess to secrets she had no right to know if she couldn't handle a few kisses.

He ran his hand from her neck down her arm and back up again. He kissed her, savoring her plump mouth, nibbling along the edges, as he pushed her backward to recline on the sofa. He traced the juncture of her lips, nudging them to open just as she softly landed on the leather cushion. He deepened the kiss, thrusting his tongue inside her mouth and expecting her to shove him off and bolt to her room.

Instead she brought her hands to his shoulders and began a light exploration as he deepened the kiss one notch further. He could feel the tentative touch of her small hands and cursed the fabric of his shirt, wishing she actually had her hands on him.

Oh, no! No. No. No. That was not the way this was supposed to go. She was not supposed to do things that made him want her her way. He was supposed to be…warning her. Pushing her. Showing her that his abundant experience made them incompatible. So he wouldn't have to admit the obvious: That he couldn't be faithful no matter how wonderful she was.

He yanked his mind away from enjoying the touch of her hands on him, and back to proving they were incompatible, as he combed his fingers through the soft silk of her hair. Warmth curled in low in his belly. Everything about her was soft, whispery, feminine, and he wondered fleetingly if that wasn't why she appealed to him. He had never met anyone as naturally soft and beautiful as she was, not just physically, but also personally. He loved her sweetness. He sipped at it now, took it into him, and felt so loved he could have died from the sheer pleasure of it.

And he suddenly recognized the truth of that. She loved him. And he wanted that love. Innocent. Pure. Honest. He *wanted* it.

She began to undo the buttons of his shirt and Jake realized he had already undone most of the buttons on her blouse. A habit? An instinct? He wasn't sure which. But something had him doing the things he wanted to do without even thinking about them.

He glanced down at her. She smiled and a swell of emotion rose up in him. He couldn't believe how beautiful she was. How perfect. He studied the features of her face, then let his gaze cruise from her jaw down her slim neck and along her collar to the place where he had separated buttons. A soft wisp of lace snaked across the pearly white skin of her breast.

He caught her gaze again. "You're perfect."

She smiled. "You're perfect."

And she wasn't afraid. That was clear.

And he wanted this. That was also clear.

But it was wrong. He had been trying to demonstrate that to her, trying to show that his experience made them sexually incompatible. He was supposed to fill her with so much fear that she bolted from the room and never tempted him again. Instead she had fed him with sweetness. She had slowed him down. She had shown him emotion. And she had turned the tables. She had brought him to a dimension of love and sex where he had never been before. He wanted it so much he could taste it, but he also knew he wouldn't keep it. He would be his own worst enemy.

He squeezed his eyes shut. "We can't do this." He shifted himself away from her and off the couch. "We cannot do this!"

Before she could say a word of protest, he was the one who bolted from the room.

Chapter Ten

The next morning Hannah poured a cup of coffee to take to Jake in his office. She wasn't disheartened by his running out on her the night before. She knew something haunted him. But from what they had been doing before he remembered it, she also believed there was hope for them. She had to be patient. But she also had to keep himself in front of him so much that he realized their being together was inevitable. She had to make him see he could trust her and that they could fix whatever haunted him.

Walking down the corridor to his office, Hannah felt very good about her plan and very confident. She stepped through the open door, steaming mug of coffee in hand, ready to greet him, but he wasn't at his desk. His computer was on so she assumed he must have been here, but then she remembered that his computer had been on the night before and he had been too upset about nearly making love to think to turn it off.

She smiled at the memory of how he almost couldn't resist making love on his office sofa, but didn't dwell on it because the way he was beginning to trust her was more important than their sexual attraction. She walked toward his desk, trying to decide if she should leave the coffee, a warm reminder that she wanted to care for him and be part of his life, or if she should go back to the kitchen and wait for a sign that he really was awake so it wouldn't get cold.

She decided to leave the coffee and placed the steaming mug on a coaster. She turned away, but curiosity overwhelmed her and she turned again. She didn't want to put her nose in where it didn't belong, but she was curious about him. And he didn't tell her much. Besides, maybe something she saw here could help her.

She rounded the desk and without much more than a cursory glance, she recognized the papers on his desk to be prospectus for investments, annual statements from companies he was apparently considering investing in and junk mail. She sighed, telling herself she wasn't going to learn anything here and began to walk away, but as she passed his computer, she ran her fingers lightly over the keyboard. Immediately, the screen saver disappeared and onto the monitor popped a picture of the nursery.

She stopped. The nursery?

Confused, she stared at it for a few seconds until she realized from the way Dixon's billowing curtains were blowing in the light morning breeze that the picture was in real time. This wasn't another screen saver. It wasn't a picture. Jake had a camera on the nursery.

She fell to the tall-backed black leather chair behind her. Studying the scene on the monitor, she realized the camera was positioned so that he could see everything. It telecast a view from the changing table by the door, to the toy box on the other side of the room. That, of course, took in the crib, which was centered against the back wall. The only thing she couldn't see was the shelf of toys. From the look of the picture, it was clear that one of the toys on the eye-level shelf housed the camera.

She licked her dry lips and her heart, which felt as if it had stopped, suddenly leaped into overdrive.

He had been spying on her!

She tried to tell herself that he could have been monitoring Dixon, and she believed that until she realized that the fact that the program was open and running meant he had been watching last night. Probably right before she came in the room. Which meant Jake was monitoring her performance with Dixon.

She tried to tell herself that was normal. That a parent who traveled would be concerned about a baby with a new nanny, but she had been working for him for weeks! And he was home! It wasn't as though he was monitoring his son's life while he was away. He was home! There was no reason to spy! If he wanted to see how Dixon was doing, all he had to do was come upstairs to the nursery!

Indignation sputtered through her.

She blew her breath out in an angry huff of air. Everything she felt for him, everything she had been trying to do for him, suddenly felt cheap. Worthless. Fraudulent.

"Hannah don't!"

Hearing Jake's voice from the doorway, Hannah spun his chair around to face him. She could tell from the set of his shoulders that he was tense, primed for a fight. Well, by God, she would give him one!

"Don't what? Don't spy on what's going on in the nursery? I would think as the baby's nanny I would have every reason in the world to see what's going on in the nursery. After all, as Dixon's primary caregiver, I should be as concerned as you are… In fact, in *fairness*," she said, emphasizing the word fairness, "wouldn't it have been smart to tell me about the camera? That way, when I wanted to check on Dixon, I could do it without going upstairs and risking waking him. Unless the camera really isn't to check on Dixon, but to check up on me."

"Hannah," he said soothingly as he stepped into the room. "It's not exactly what you think."

"Really?" she asked, anger bubbling so high now that she felt she would choke on it. To think she had felt so much love for him she ached to help him. She thought last night meant they trusted each other. "Then what is it?"

"At first—I have to admit—I was concerned about my son. You can't fault a man who has to travel for wanting to know what's going on in his house…with his child while he's gone."

Already having admitted that to herself, Hannah could concede that, but it wasn't the real bottom line and they both knew it. "But you trust me now," she said, meeting his gaze. "At least, I thought you trusted me. Apparently, I was wrong."

The sad look that formed in his eyes nearly did her in. She felt herself weakening and cursed herself for being a fool. She tried to run from the office, too full of anger and pain to deal with him right now.

He caught her by the arms and stopped her. "No. You're not wrong. I *do* trust you."

"Then explain this!"

"I was… I… Hannah." He squeezed his eyes shut. "I know I'm not the best dad. I know that a lot of the stuff that's supposed to come naturally to other guys didn't come to me."

"So you spied on *me?*"

"I listened to what you told Dixon about what you thought I should do to become a good dad."

That confused her so much, her tone softened. "You listened to what I told Dixon?"

"You were always telling Dixon things like 'if your daddy would spend more time with you, he would be a good dad… If your daddy would go to single dad school, he would get more confident… If your daddy would learn to care for you himself, you would be able to spend more time together…' And every time you said one of them you were right. Every time I took your advice I grew as a father. I didn't have a role model. You might be too young to remember this, but my dad left my mom three years before he died." He combed his fingers through his hair. "It just seemed like the right thing to do at the time."

Hannah blinked back tears. It was all so confusing. Everything was tied in with something else. He used the camera to learn to be a good dad, but she had thought his becoming a good dad was a sign he was changing, learning, growing, and that they shared some kind of supernatural communication. Instead he had only been taking advice she had been giving him. Which meant he hadn't been changing, meant that he wasn't intuitive with her… And meant he didn't love her. Maybe even *couldn't* love her.

"You didn't come up with any of these ideas on your own?" she asked desperately, managing to whisper through a throat clogged with tears.

He shook his head. "No."

"You spied on me? Invaded my privacy?"

"The supreme court might disagree with that interpretation."

Though she felt like a complete fool for thinking he was changing and an even bigger fool for thinking they shared some kind of mystic chemistry, she met his gaze again. She could feel tears shimmering on her eyelids and prayed they wouldn't spill over, but also knew she had to do this. She had to take this discussion to its honest conclusion so she would get it through her thick skull once and for all this man did not want her.

"This isn't about the supreme court...or any court. This is about us, personally, about trust."

"I do trust you."

"No." She shook her head sadly. "You don't."

Saying that out loud caused it to sink in the way Hannah wanted it to, and her entire world felt as if it was falling in on her. She could see how all the assumptions she had made over the past few weeks weren't based on anything more than her own wishful thinking. She could see that she had attributed characteristics to him that he didn't have because she wanted him to have them.

She licked her dry lips, ready to say something— what, she wasn't sure—but was saved from that by the ringing doorbell.

Though her entire body resonated with emotion, her work ethic was alive and well and saving her right now. "I'd better get that."

Jake gripped her shoulders. "No. It can't be that important. It's probably just a deliveryman. This is more important."

But as far as Hannah was concerned their discussion was over and the door was a hundred times more important, because it was her way out of his office. She shook her head and shook his hands off her shoulders, but he caught her before she could escape.

"Please, Hannah!"

She shook him off again. "No. Jake. Damn it! I don't understand what's happening here, but I do know it changes everything." And it also broke her heart. She had built him into something he wasn't because it was what she wanted him to be. Because she wanted him to love her, because she loved him. Desperately. Honestly. With every fiber of her being, she loved him.

She was such a fool.

"I don't want to talk about this anymore." She pushed past him as the doorbell rang again. "I'm getting that."

"Hannah!" he called, running after her to try to stop her. Unfortunately she was quicker than he was and she slipped from his grasp and made it to the front door before he could catch her. She opened it and Felicity pushed her way inside.

"Damn it! Jake! How the hell long were you going to make me stand there and ring that bell?"

Though Jake appeared too stunned to speak, in her already numb state Hannah felt a cool detachment taking over. She noticed that Felicity wasn't just beautiful, she was breathtaking. Her long red hair caressed the porcelain skin of her back and shoulders, both of which were exposed by the low-cut sundress she wore.

Her blue eyes could have given the devil weak knees. Her figure had been blessed by the gods.

Knowing Jake had been involved with Felicity, but never married her, even though they had a son, Hannah suddenly wondered how the hell she ever thought Jake Malloy would want a simple small-town teacher when he had blown off a goddess. Just in terms of looks, Hannah could not compete with the women in Jake's life.

"I've come for Dixon."

"What?"

Felicity faced Jake with a brilliant smile. "I've come for Dixon. I'm ready to take him home."

Jake stared at her for a few seconds before he said, "But I thought you had another two months of filming?"

"All the location shots are done, so we've set up shop at the studio in L.A. Dixon and I can go home."

"But…"

Tears sprang to Hannah's eyes as her second mortal blow of the day landed. Not only was she losing the fairy-tale fantasy she had created around Jake, but also, she was losing Dixon. Her heart expanded with pain, but along with it came an awful sense of truth that she had been ignoring for the past weeks. Dixon was not her son. She shouldn't have allowed herself to get so attached. Once again, she was the cause of her own misery. And there was nothing for her to fight. She had no grounds to keep Dixon. She had a made a big mistake in getting so attached to him.

Miserable, she turned toward the stairway. "I'll go pack his things, get him dressed."

Jake grabbed her arm. "Hannah, no!"

"What do you mean, no!" Felicity said, grabbing

Jake's arm and spinning him away from Hannah. "I have to be on the set tomorrow morning. I have just enough time to get myself home, get rid of some of this jet lag and be on the set tomorrow at seven. We're going *now*."

Jake combed his hands through his hair. "Felicity, you can't just dump Dixon on me then march in and demand he go back with you in a split second."

"I think that as the person with custody I can."

"You don't have custody. We never finalized that. We never formalized it."

Felicity gasped. "What are you saying?"

Jake combed his fingers through his hair. "I don't know."

Hannah turned toward the stairs again and began climbing. Jake had an interesting, exciting life, very different from anything Hannah had ever experienced. He had people in his life who were interesting, exciting, beautiful. She didn't belong.

She marched up the steps and prepared to pack Dixon to leave, but changed her mind. The baby was asleep. She wasn't about to wake him when his parents were fighting and might fight for the next several hours. There was no point in waking him. No point in packing his clothes. And no point in her staying anymore.

Numb, saddened to her very core, she turned and walked to her room. She stuffed her few belongings into her suitcase, made one last trip to Dixon's room to say goodbye, then she sneaked down the back stairs to the kitchen. She didn't bother writing Jake a note. He was a smart guy. In a minute or two he would realize it no longer mattered that she was angry about the NannyCam, because she wasn't his nanny anymore. And what was done was done. They could argue that problem from here to the supreme court, but it wouldn't make any difference now. Her tenure as his nanny was over. He would probably be glad she had gone.

Tears trembled on her eyelids as she took one last look around. In the recesses of her subconscious, she had thought this was home. She had thought of Dixon as her own. She had thought Jake loved her. But he didn't. He couldn't. He was from a completely different world than she was. He believed in spying on nannies instead of trusting them. He got his son unconventionally. He traveled the globe at whim.

She definitely didn't fit. Not only was it time to face that, but it was time to make herself a place in the world where she did fit. She wasn't a kid anymore. Surviving this pain, this embarrassment, would officially shove her into the world of adults.

Jake watched Hannah driving out of the lane that led to his house and he almost bolted after her. Almost.

Hannah was a grown woman who was justifiably angry with him. Dixon was a baby, with the oddest parents on the face of the earth. His mother wanted to be a movie star. His dad was being recruited by the CIA. Both were reaching their goals at the same time. And Dixon was the one who would end up stranded because of it.

For thirty seconds Jake considered abandoning the CIA in favor of raising Dixon, but he knew babies belonged with their mothers. Besides, without Hannah, he couldn't care for his son on his own.

He scrubbed his hand down his face and headed for the steps. "Come on, help me get Dixon packed."

"I thought that girl was getting him packed."

Jake turned, faced her. "That *girl* was Hannah Evans, Dixon's nanny while he was here. And she left." The words echoed through his empty foyer and twisted a knife in Jake's heart. But he reminded himself he couldn't have Hannah any more than he could keep Dixon. Impossible as it sounded, Felicity had a more stable life than Jake did. She had a full-time professional nanny. The bigger a star she became, the further in advance she would know her plans. And the more capable of caring for Dixon she would become. While Jake's life would always be up in the air.

The phone rang just as Jake stepped into the nursery and from the ring, he knew it was his private line, the line for which only Edgar had the number.

"I have to get that." He pointed at the white dresser. "Hannah had most of Dixon's things in those drawers. His diaper bags and duffels are in the closet."

He turned to leave the nursery just as Dixon sat up in the crib. "Dad!" he yelled.

Jake stopped dead in his tracks. Unexpected, unbridled emotion overwhelmed him. Not only had his son spoken, but he recognized him and he needed him. He didn't want him to leave.

Jake faced the crib again. "Dad?"

"Dad, dad, dad, dad, dad," Dixon said, patting his palms against his chubby thighs.

"Oh, he's just making sounds," Felicity said, then she laughed. "Don't get all excited, thinking he said dad before he said mom."

"He did say dad," Jake said, returning to the room.

He gazed at his son incredulously. "Dixon, you said dad."

"Dad, dad, dad…"

The phone rang again.

"You're an idiot, Jake," Felicity said with another airy laugh. "Go get your phone."

Dixon said, "Brrr, brrr, bree," with the same tone and enthusiasm as he had said "Dad, dad, dad," and Jake took a long breath. The moment was over and Felicity appeared to be right.

"I'll just go get the phone," Jake said, and headed for the door. He ran to his bedroom and grabbed that extension. "Hello?"

"Hey!" Edgar said, a chuckle in his voice. "You're out of breath! Don't tell me that now that I've finally seen your potential, you're getting old on me."

"You're the one who took ten years to realize I was right under your nose. It would be your fault if I had gotten old in the process."

"Well, don't get any older because we need you."

Jake heard the tone that crept into Edgar's voice and he sat on his bed. "You need me?"

"Yeah. But my supervisors and I have changed our minds about how we want to use you."

"How?"

"The fact that you tripped over your fake name in Belgium proved you probably aren't agent material."

"I see." Jake ran his hand down his face. This day just kept getting better and better. Could he lose anything else? Did he have anything else to lose? Hannah was gone. Dixon was going. Now the job that was supposed to give him adventure was going up in smoke.

Edgar laughed. "I don't think you do see. You

might not be agent material, but the way we want to use you is more dangerous because you would have to be yourself.''

''I don't understand.''

''You know that our operations require us to set up people with fake identities. You gave credence to one of them simply by pretending to be someone's brother. But you can be even more effective as yourself. You would go into a scene as the friend of the person our agent is portraying and when you're checked you don't just show up as an SAT score, college transcript or credit record, you are actually in the newspapers.''

Jake quietly said, ''Yes, I am.''

''The thing of it is, though, we want you to quit Sunbright and working with Troy Cramer altogether. It's a great cover for your travel, but it jeopardizes Troy's company and his reputation, if you're somehow caught and accused of something. It also works better for us if you can establish yourself internationally somehow. Get a reputation as a gambler, a partier, a skier, a tennis bum. Anything. That way you can travel at whim and no one questions why you're going anywhere.''

Jake said, ''I see what you're saying.''

''I thought you would. And I also think this is a much better way for you to use your talents.''

''So do I.''

''Good.''

With that Edgar hung up the phone and Jake stared at it in astonishment.

He was in. He was really in. Not a spy, not an agent, but someone every bit as important. Himself.

The only things he had lost today were his son and Hannah.

He squeezed his eyes shut. He had to stop thinking like that. Dixon was in better hands with Felicity and he'd never had Hannah.

You cannot lose what you do not have.

He entered the nursery and found Felicity standing by the crib, chatting with Dixon, who laughed merrily with her.

"You didn't pack."

She turned to him with a confused look on her face. "Jake, you know I don't do things like pack."

"It's not hard, Felicity!"

"I didn't say it was. I just said I don't do stuff like that. That's why we have people. You shouldn't have let your girl get away."

He scowled at her, hating the way he referred to Hannah as if she were a second-class citizen and feeling his heart break one more time because he had let her get away. But he had to! He didn't have a choice.

He picked up the duffel bag and began shoving Dixon's things inside. Felicity went back to playing with the baby, but, Jake noticed, she didn't touch him.

"Have you checked his diaper?"

Felicity gasped and spun to face him. "Of course not!"

"Felicity, he's been napping. He's probably soaked. Change him while I pack."

"Absolutely not!"

Jake only stared at her until realization dawned. "You've never changed his diaper?"

She looked horrified at the thought. "No!"

"How about fed him?"

"The nanny does that."

"Have you ever touched him at all?"

"Of course, I have. Don't be ridiculous and stop

trying to make me out to be a bad mother. I love Dixon. I'm just not a motherly type."

Yeah, Jake could see that. And he could also see something else. He might not be able to be a permanent dad, but he couldn't abandon Dixon to Felicity. He had to take a more active role in his son's life, albeit worked in around his CIA assignments.

"What would you say if I told you I was thinking of moving to L.A.?"

Again Felicity spun to face him. "Really? I thought you loved it here in Podunkville."

"I did. I do… But Dixon has to come first. I thought that if I got a place close enough to yours I could have Dixon more."

Felicity smiled broadly. "You would move to L.A. just to be near the baby?"

Jake took a long breath.

She thought about that a second, then shrugged. "Hey, works for me."

"It works for me, too," Jake said, because it did. He had nothing to hold him here, not even Hannah. Undoubtedly, she would be on her way out of town as soon as she got her things packed.

But at least he still had Dixon. That was enough. He would make it enough.

Chapter Eleven

As Jake was packing his briefcase on Monday morning, Troy entered his office. "Hey, going somewhere?"

"Actually, I am."

"Where?"

"On a business trip that doesn't have anything to do with our investments or Sunbright."

"Oh."

"Troy, would you close the door so we could talk for a bit?"

"You're quitting, aren't you?" Troy said as he shut the door and turned to face Jake again.

Jake took a long breath. "Yes."

"It's okay," Troy said, and fell into the seat in front of Jake's desk. "I had been mentally preparing myself for this but I'm suddenly not as ready as I thought I would be."

"You knew I would be quitting?"

"Jake, I knew the CIA was going to recruit you long before you did."

Jake only stared at Troy.

"What? Do you think the CIA, which depends on me and this company to periodically check equipment, software and ideas is going to steal my right-hand person and not run it by me first? Do you think they would use you, and by association, my company, for pickups and deliveries and not tell me?"

When Troy put it that way, it did seem a little naive of Jake to believe that. "So, now you're going to try to talk me out of it?"

Troy shook his head. "You wouldn't have made the decision to work for them unless you had a good reason. A person would have to be foolish to try to stop you. But I just want to ask, what about Dixon?"

"I'm moving to L.A. to spend more time with Dixon. That's actually why I'm quitting my job. The CIA assignments will be few and far between. I'm just a person who drops in to lend credence to a real agent's story." He laughed slightly. "I have no illusions about being a spy. I'm just window dressing."

"But important window dressing if your presence lends authenticity to an agent's cover."

Jake sighed with relief at Troy's understanding. "Yes."

"And you don't need money anymore. So you're basically free to do anything you want."

Jake laughed. "Thanks to you."

"No. The credit goes to you. You earned us both a fortune in the years we invested together." Troy rose. "So, this is goodbye, then?"

"Yes. I'm leaving my house with my mother and stepfather to keep or sell. I don't care. I'll arrange for movers to pack and ship my clothes and personal belongings so that after this quick assignment I can get set up in my new house in Los Angeles. I'm going to help raise my son. He needs me. Felicity doesn't have a maternal bone in her body and Hannah taught me a lot.''

"What about Hannah?"

"What about Hannah?"

Troy caught Jake's gaze. "Aren't you going to say goodbye?"

Jake busied himself with stacking some papers. "Hannah and I said our goodbyes."

"I don't call an argument over a NannyCam saying goodbye."

Not surprised that Hannah would have told that part of the story to explain why she wasn't working for him anymore, Jake said, "It's going to have to be."

"Afraid?"

Jake paused, pursed his lips, and considered lying through his teeth. Instead he looked his best friend in the eye. "No, I just don't think it's appropriate for someone with my past to settle down with someone like Hannah."

"Is that how you really feel?"

"Yes."

"I'm not sure you're correct, but if it's how you feel then you're doing the right thing." Troy opened the office door. "I'll call you for dinner when Sadie and I are in L.A. next month."

"Great!" Jake said, realizing that moving away wouldn't be so bad after all. He would see Sadie and Troy regularly and friends from Sunbright who traveled to California.

He wouldn't be leaving anybody behind except Hannah.

And he knew that was why there was a hole in his heart.

But it would mend. He was sure it would mend. He had a son and a part in saving the world—a purpose for his life. It would be greedy and foolish to reach for anything more.

And cruel. If he were to marry Hannah and then couldn't be faithful, it would break her heart.

Better to forget all about her.

Jake sat in the dining room of a home nestled in the periphery of a heat-soaked Colombian jungle. Cocaine country. Word had been spread that he had quit working for Sunbright Solutions and dissolved his investment partnership with Troy because he no longer needed money. Which was true.

The second half of the story was also somewhat true. Because he no longer had a job he was free to travel, party and have indiscriminate sexual liaisons. Like the one he was supposedly having with his hostess, Rachel McIntyre. That was his calling card into her home for her three-person dinner party.

Though Rachel, a spitfire redhead, was a real agent, her cover was that of a socialite whose family had lost its fortune. Unwilling or unable to live a normal life, Rachel had cooked up the scheme of becoming a cocaine link between her jet-setter friends and the cartel she was currently wooing. The CIA had no intention of busting the drug ring. They were tracking money, making sure none of this Cartel's fortune went to terrorists. Jake's entire purpose was to arrive at her house, stay long enough for the cartel to realize he was worth investigating, and then validate her existence as a jet-setter simply by the fact that Jake's story would check.

Rachel had already told Jake she intended to keep the "business" conversations away from the dinner table. Not just to protect Jake, but also to prove to the general dining with them that she was serious. Jake was more than willing to go along with that, because the general was a huge, evil-looking man who Jake knew wouldn't hesitate to kill them both if he suspected they were CIA.

But through the dinner conversation, which revolved around the general's hunting prowess, Jake's mind drifted to Hannah. He knew Dixon was in good hands with the L.A. nanny and would be in better hands once Jake returned to his new home. But as Troy had said, he had never really had closure with Hannah. Not that he wanted some big discussion. He knew that wouldn't solve anything. But he would like to see the look in her shiny green eyes when she told him of her new job, her first apartment, her new friends. He scowled. Not her male friends—though he knew she would have male friends, tons of them. Not because he'd helped her shop and introduced her to Anton, but because she was beautiful and sweet and wonderful.

His hands gripped the edge of the table.

"A problem, Mr. Malloy?" the general said with a laugh.

Caught woolgathering, Jake knew this was one of the times when the truth was better than lying, and another way he could prove himself to be real and validate Rachel.

"Just a woman in the States who makes me crazy."

"Ah."

Rachel smiled. "Jake has a son."

"And his mother is your problem?"

Jake started to answer, but Rachel beat him to it. "No. Jake got a little too personal with the family nanny."

"Oh, *señor!*" The general laughed heartily. "One should either know better or know to be discreet."

Jake's eyes narrowed as he stared at Rachel. She had probably made that up out of thin air, but the insult of it struck too close to home. Hannah was not that kind of girl.

"It wasn't like that," Jake mumbled.

"Fall in love?" the general asked.

"Yeah, Jake," Rachel asked, leaning her elbow on the padded arm of her chair and giving him her attention the way a casual lover would as she grilled him about his escapades. "Did you fall in love? Do you even know what love is? Can any of us know what love is?" she asked. She wasn't talking philosophy as much as she was trying to further the scam she was perpetrating that she and Jake were lovers.

But the truth was she had hit Jake's problem on the head. He really had gotten personal with his child's nanny. He really had let her go because he hadn't wanted to hurt her. Except, he couldn't forget her. And this job, which was supposed to give his life meaning, was actually kind of boring.

Just as Jake thought the last, a burst of gunfire pelted the room. The general was hit and fell forward. Rachel gasped and dropped to the floor, ducking under the table. Jake scrambled to join her.

"What the hell!" Jake said, but Rachel silenced him.

"Shut up. We're fine. I could tell from the gunfire there was one shooter. I'm guessing this was an assassination."

"Holy sh—"

"Shh-hh," Rachel said as she scrambled to pull a small gun from a garter belt. "I'm going to check on things."

Before she got the final word out of her mouth, gunfire filled the air again.

"Shoot!" Rachel fell back beside him on the floor. "Do you have a cell phone?"

"Yeah, but…"

She grabbed it from his hand, hit a few buttons and then dialed a number. "Get in here. We've been compromised."

Jake stared at her. "You said that over a cell phone!"

"We're compromised! It doesn't matter! Our only goal now is to get the hell out of here alive."

Another burst of gunfire blew over their heads and Jake suddenly realized he could be killed. He leaned back against the table leg and two things struck him. If he died, he would be leaving Dixon alone with Felicity. Crazy, wacky, not even slightly maternal Felicity.

And if he died, he would never get to tell Hannah he loved her, never get to see her in the throes of passion, never get to pretend to like her cooking, or never get to wake up with her nestled against him.

Worse, he would leave Hannah without the love of her life—and *he was* the love of her life because, by God, she was the love of his. Realizing that, he knew there wasn't a snowball's chance in hell he would be unfaithful. He loved her. He loved her more than anything. He had no explanation for his father or his life-style. All he knew was that right at this moment, his father didn't matter. If Jake got out of this he wasn't just going to tell Hannah that he loved her, he was going to marry her.

He grabbed Rachel's arm. "I'm getting out of here."

"Jake! You can't!"

"The hell I can't!" He began to crawl out from under the table. "Do you have any other guns?"

"Yes."

"Where are they?"

"All over the house, basically, but Jake you'll virtually have to crawl on your stomach to get them."

"Not a problem," he said, and meant it.

"Okay, then the easiest one to get from here is in the bottom drawer of the cabinet beside the table."

"Here in the dining room?"

"Yes."

"Then what the hell are we sitting here for!" He slid out from under the table and belly-crawled to the cabinet at the same time that he heard the noise of an approaching helicopter.

"We were sitting here waiting for our ride!" Rachel called to him. "And it's here! All we had to do was sit tight."

Jake crawled over to her. "Yeah. Well, we still have to get across the courtyard, and I think we're going to need this," he said, brandishing the automatic weapon.

"Do you know how to use that?" Rachel yelled over the sound of the helicopter.

He shook his head. "No."

She took the automatic and gave him her pistol.

"Let's go!" she yelled, and led him to the door behind a burst of her own gunfire.

As he ran, Jake scanned the area, looking for the general's assassin. Amid another burst of gunfire, Rachel jumped into the helicopter that had landed in the courtyard of her huge home. When neither of them was hit, Jake realized the gunmen were aiming for the helicopter and not them, and he jumped in, too, praying the shooter would miss the blatant target filled with combustible fuel.

An experienced agent, Rachel shoved Jake behind her and sprayed bullets on the courtyard as the helicopter rose.

Ten seconds later the only sound Jake heard was the sound of the vehicle's rotating blades and the thump, thump, thump of his own heart.

"All packed and ready to go?" Hannah's dad called as he strode up the sidewalk to the driveway where Hannah stood beside her car.

"I'm all packed, but I'm not sure I'm ready to go," Hannah said, tears stinging her eyes as she looked around, up and down the quiet street, realizing she was going to miss her town. She would miss her family, her nosy sisters, her overprotective big brother, her dad, her mother, the neighbors... Everything. Everybody. But most of all, she would miss Jake. She'd had one shot at a fabulous, once-in-a-lifetime love and she had blown it. And she wasn't even quite sure how.

Still, there was no reason for her dad to know that. She took a deep breath to stem the desire to weep uncontrollably. "I'm ready."

Lily Evans hugged her baby girl. "You be careful now."

"Mom, Sadie has given my name and address to her old police unit. I have a feeling that I'm going to have more company and more protection than a single woman really needs…" She glanced at gloating Sadie. "Or wants."

"You can never be too careful in the city," Pete Evans began, defending Sadie's actions, but a blue sports car screamed into their driveway. Even before it came to a complete stop, Jake jumped out of the driver's seat.

"What the heck," Lily said, but Jake called, "Hannah! Wait! Wait!"

"Oh, no!" Hannah said, and opened her car door. She knew Jake wasn't the 'settling down' kind, but she was also smart enough to know that she wasn't immune to him. If she let him, he could talk her into anything. She turned to jump into her car.

But Jake caught her arm and spun her around before she could get inside. "Don't go."

"Jake, I have a job. I have an apartment, and you don't need me anymore."

"I don't need you, but I do love you."

Her sisters gasped.

Sadie cooed, "Oh-hh!" but Hannah noticed Aunt Sadie catch her arm and turn her in the direction of the Evans's house. "Girls, I think we need to go inside."

Maria rubbed her hands together with glee. "I think we need to stay."

Pete caught Maria's upper arm. Lily grabbed Caro's. Before Hannah knew what happened, she and Jake were alone.

"That must have been some party," she said, plucking at his filthy tuxedo. Her gaze narrowed. "Is that blood on your shirt?"

Eyes wide, he glanced down. "No! It's ketchup. I had a hot dog at the airport."

"You were in an airport dressed like this?"

"Only to catch Troy's private plane, so I could get to you before you left."

"Well, you're too late. I have a job. I have an apartment. I'm packed and ready to go. In another two hours I'll be settled in the suburb of Wexford."

He caught her upper arms and forced her to look at him. "Do you really want to go?"

She smiled and nodded, but the dearness of his face nearly did her in. She couldn't stop herself from remembering shopping with him. The way he looked at her new haircut. The way he kissed her. She swallowed hard. "Yeah. I gotta go."

"I don't want you to go."

"You don't have a say in things."

"Not even if I ask you to marry me?"

She took a pace back and looked at his filthy, wrinkled tux again. "I don't know where you were and I don't know what you did, but don't let one overly wild party scare you into thinking you want to change your life."

"It wasn't a wild party. I can't tell you what it was. But you're going to have to trust me when I tell you that even before the gunfire began I was having second thoughts."

"Gunfire!"

"Let's just say I thought I couldn't settle down." He dropped his forehead to hers. "Because I was afraid I was like my dad. He was unfaithful to my mother." He pulled back and caught her gaze. "A lot.

I thought I would do the same thing to you. But when everything fell apart around me, everything took on a whole new perspective and I knew I wouldn't.''

She didn't say anything, only studied his face. Finally she said, "I always knew that. Now, what the hell were you doing in gunfire?"

"Putting the punctuation at the end of an already drawn conclusion. I love you, Hannah. I want to marry you. To sleep with you every night and wake up with you every morning. I even want to pretend to like your awful cooking.''

Her eyes narrowed.

"I want to raise Dixon with you…"

"What about Felicity?"

"Troy invested in a new movie project so that she could get the starring role. This is her honest-to-God big chance, so she's willing to be the parent with visitation rights, instead of the parent with custody.''

"Really?"

"Really. We would get Dixon. I would eat your awful cooking.'' He brushed his lips across hers lightly. "We could go to bed together every night, wake up together every morning.'' He kissed her again. This time more deeply. "We could make our own kids.''

She pulled away. "But you're not going to tell me about the gunfire.''

"I've already said more than I should. But I had to because you would have eventually figured out this isn't ketchup.'' He glanced down at his shirt before he caught her gaze. "But I didn't kill anybody, wasn't in a fight, and actually wasn't the target of this particular situation.''

She started to laugh. "You really had one hell of a life going, didn't you?"

"I wasn't a bomber, wasn't in organized crime, have never killed anybody, don't want to kill anybody, and can't remember the last time I was even in a fist-fight."

She put her finger over his lips to stop his jabbering, rose to her tiptoes and kissed him. "Okay."

He went perfectly still. "Okay, you believe me?"

She shook her head. "No. Okay, I'll marry you."

"You will?"

"Yes. I'm not sure if it's a good thing or a bad thing that you had to be in a life-and-death situation before you could decide to marry me, but I'll take you anyway."

He looped his arms around her and pulled her close. "I had actually decided before the life-and-death situation."

"So you said."

"But have I told you that I love you?"

"Yeah, but I could stand to hear it about fifty million more times."

"And you will." He released her slightly and looked into her eyes. "You drove me crazy. Then the decision to leave you about tore me in two. But in the end, when I faced life without you, I knew I couldn't do it."

"Bingo. That's the kind of stuff you're supposed to say when you propose."

"Then let's go tell your parents."

She nuzzled into his neck. "Let's go back to your house and finish what we started on the sofa of your office a few weeks ago."

He paused, considered that, and realized she was

talking about how she had almost seduced him there the night before she left.

"Better idea," he said, and turned her toward his car. "Much, much better idea."

* * * * *

*This September 2003, be sure
to look for Susan Meier's next romance,*

LOVE, YOUR SECRET ADMIRER,

*the first title in Silhouette Romance's
exciting new six-book series,*

MARRYING THE BOSS'S DAUGHTER.

Helen R. Myers
No Sanctuary

Where do you go when there's no place to hide?

Metal sculptor Bay Butler spent six years in a Texas prison for a crime she did not commit—until the efforts of a powerful client get her conviction overturned. Suddenly Bay is free, but she is still plagued with questions. Why was she imprisoned based on circumstantial evidence? And what really happened the night her business partner was found brutally murdered in their studio?

Her quest for the truth brings her face-to-face with Jack Burke, the cop who arrested her for the murder. Bay Butler's case has haunted him for six years—and so has the woman herself. Together they embark on a trail of deadly secrets that threaten the foundation of a small Texas town...a town where power and money have exacted a price in blood.

Available the first week of May 2003, wherever paperbacks are sold!

We're proud to present two emotional novels of strong Western passions, intense, irresistible heroes and the women who are about to tear down their walls of protection!

Don't miss

SUMMER
Gold

containing

Sweet Wind, Wild Wind
by *New York Times* bestselling author
Elizabeth Lowell

&

A Wolf River Summer
an original novel by
Barbara McCauley

Available this June wherever Silhouette books are sold.

Silhouette®
Where love comes alive™

Don't miss the latest miniseries from award-winning author Marie Ferrarella:

Meet...

Sherry Campbell—ambitious newswoman who makes headlines when a handsome billionaire arrives to sweep her off her feet...and shepherd her new son into the world!
A BILLIONAIRE AND A BABY, SE#1528,
available March 2003

Joanna Prescott—Nine months after her visit to the sperm bank, her old love rescues her from a burning house—then delivers her baby....
A BACHELOR AND A BABY, SD#1503,
available April 2003

Chris "C.J." Jones—FBI agent, expectant mother and always on the case. When the baby comes, will her irresistible partner be by her side?
THE BABY MISSION, IM#1220, available May 2003

Lori O'Neill—A forbidden attraction blows down this pregnant Lamaze teacher's tough-woman facade and makes her consider the love of a lifetime!
BEAUTY AND THE BABY, SR#1668,
available June 2003

The Mom Squad—these single mothers-to-be are ready for labor...and true love!

Where love comes alive™

SILHOUETTE *Romance*

COMING NEXT MONTH

#1666 PREGNANT BY THE BOSS!—Carol Grace

Champagne under the mistletoe had led to more than kisses for tycoon Joe Callaway and his assistant. Unwilling to settle for less than true love, Claudia Madison left him on reluctant feet. Could Joe win Claudia back in time to hear the pitter-patter of new ones?

#1667 BETROTHED TO THE PRINCE—Raye Morgan

Catching the Crown

Sometimes the beautiful princess needed to dump her never-met betrothed—at least that's what independent Tianna Roseanova-Krimorova thought. But a mystery baby, a mistaken identity and a surprisingly sexy prince soon made her wonder if fairy-tale endings weren't so bad after all!

#1668 BEAUTY AND THE BABY—Marie Ferrarella

The Mom Squad

Widowed, broke and pregnant, Lori O'Neill longed for a knight. And along came...*her brother-in-law?* Carson O'Neill had always done the right thing. But the sweet seductress made this Mr. Nice Guy think about being very, very naughty!

#1669 A GIFT FROM THE PAST—Carla Cassidy

Soulmates

Could Joshua McCane and his estranged wife ever agree on anything? But Claire needed his help, so he reluctantly offered his services. Soon, their desire for each other threatened to rage out of control. Was Joshua so sure their love was gone?

#1670 TUTORING TUCKER—Debrah Morris

The headline: "West Texas Oil Field Foreman Brandon Tucker Wins $50 Million, Hires Saucy, Sexy Trust Fund Socialite To Teach Him The Finer Things In Life." The *Finer Things* course study: candlelight kisses, slow, sensual waltzes, velvety soft caresses...

#1671 OOPS...WE'RE MARRIED?—SUSAN LUTE

When career-driven Eleanor Rose wanted to help charity, she wrote a check. She did *not* marry a man who wanted a mother for his son and a comfortable wife for himself. She did *not* become Suzy Homemaker...*nor* give in to seductive glances... or passionate kisses...or fall in love. Or did she?

SRCNM0503